RESCUED BY LOVE

She had not gone far when one of the men who had spoken to Ivor before dinner joined her.

"I am the odd man out tonight," he began, "so I thought I would come and find you."

He was the one Weena had taken a dislike to and she knew that her mother would have thought him common.

Equally there was something about him which told her that he was not a particularly attractive person and she really had no desire to be with him.

"As it so happens," she replied to him, "I was just going to bed. I feel rather tired. Perhaps it's the fresh air and I know that I will fall asleep at once."

He then said almost in a whisper,

"If you really intend to go to bed and not talk to me as I would very much like you to do, you must at least kiss me goodnight."

Weena felt shocked by his forward behaviour and therefore said quickly,

"Goodnight. I really must go to my cabin."

He put out his arm and pulled her close to him.

"You'll go when I let you go," he insisted. "You're very pretty, in fact the prettiest girl in the whole ship. I want you to stay here with me!"

Weena put her hands against him and tried to push him away, but he was very much taller than she was and obviously much stronger.

THE BARBARA CARTLAND PINK COLLECTION

Titles in this series

RESCUED BY LOVE

BARBARA CARTLAND

Barbaracartland.com Ltd

THE BARBARA CARTLAND PINK COLLECTION

Dame Barbara Cartland is still regarded as the most prolific bestselling author in the history of the world.

In her lifetime she was frequently in the Guinness Book of Records for writing more books than any other living author.

Her most amazing literary feat was to double her output from 10 books a year to over 20 books a year when she was 77 to meet the huge demand.

She went on writing continuously at this rate for 20 years and wrote her very last book at the age of 97, thus completing an incredible 400 books between the ages of 77 and 97.

Her publishers finally could not keep up with this phenomenal output, so at her death in 2000 she left behind an amazing 160 unpublished manuscripts, something that no other author has ever achieved.

Barbara's son, Ian McCorquodale, together with his daughter Iona, felt that it was their sacred duty to publish all these titles for Barbara's millions of admirers all over the world who so love her wonderful romances.

So in 2004 they started publishing the 160 brand new Barbara Cartlands as *The Barbara Cartland Pink Collection*, as Barbara's favourite colour was always pink – and yet more pink!

The Barbara Cartland Pink Collection is published monthly exclusively by Barbaracartland.com and the books are numbered in sequence from 1 to 160.

Enjoy receiving a brand new Barbara Cartland book each month by taking out an annual subscription to the Pink Collection, or purchase the books individually.

The Pink Collection is available from the Barbara Cartland website www.barbaracartland.com via mail order and through all good bookshops.

In addition Ian and Iona are proud to announce that The Barbara Cartland Pink Collection is now available in ebook format as from Valentine's Day 2011.

For more information, please contact us at:

Barbaracartland.com Ltd.
Camfield Place
Hatfield
Hertfordshire AL9 6JE
United Kingdom

Telephone: +44 (0)1707 642629
Fax: +44 (0)1707 663041
Email: info@barbaracartland.com

THE LATE DAME BARBARA CARTLAND

Barbara Cartland who sadly died in May 2000 at the age of nearly 99 was the world's most famous romantic novelist who wrote 723 books in her lifetime with worldwide sales of over 1 billion copies and her books were translated into 36 different languages.

As well as romantic novels, she wrote historical biographies, 6 autobiographies, theatrical plays, books of advice on life, love, vitamins and cookery. She also found time to be a political speaker and television and radio personality.

She wrote her first book at the age of 21 and this was called *Jigsaw*. It became an immediate bestseller and sold 100,000 copies in hardback and was translated into 6 different languages. She wrote continuously throughout her life, writing bestsellers for an astonishing 76 years. Her books have always been immensely popular in the United States, where in 1976 her current books were at numbers 1 & 2 in the B. Dalton bestsellers list, a feat never achieved before or since by any author.

Barbara Cartland became a legend in her own lifetime and will be best remembered for her wonderful romantic novels, so loved by her millions of readers throughout the world.

Her books will always be treasured for their moral message, her pure and innocent heroines, her good looking and dashing heroes and above all her belief that the power of love is more important than anything else in everyone's life.

"Love is so strong and powerful that it can rescue you from anything however unpleasant and degrading."

Barbara Cartland

CHAPTER ONE
1895

It was growing very dark and it was difficult for the two people climbing up the mountain to see ahead clearly.

"I cannot imagine why you are taking me here," the girl kept saying.

The man merely replied,

"Come on, hurry! I want you to get to the top."

They climbed further in silence.

Then with a sigh of relief she realised that she had reached the top of that particular mountain, although there were others nearby that were higher still.

Their tips, covered with snow, reached towards the stars.

She sunk down almost exhausted and sighed,

"I cannot imagine, Ivor, why you have brought me here at this time of night. I will be very tired tomorrow."

"I want you to look down below you," Ivor replied.

She wondered what he was talking about.

But because she was feeling breathless she was not prepared to argue with him.

She looked below to where she could just see the outline of their big house and the extensive garden beyond it.

It looked to her as it always had done, an isolated building on flat land that slipped down for several miles before it reached the sea.

Then to her surprise she could see lights at what she knew was the entrance to the drive, which was bordered, almost in English fashion, with trees on either side of it.

Now she could see lights moving between them.

"Look!" she exclaimed in astonishment. "There are lights going up the drive! Who can it be and why are they going to the house at this time of night?"

"That is what I brought you up here to see," her brother answered.

"But surely we should be there to receive them?" the girl questioned. "You know that Papa cannot do so and there will only be the servants in the house."

"I think, if they are wise, the servants will already have left," her brother commented.

"What are you talking about?" the girl, whose name was Weena, asked. "I just don't understand, Ivor."

"You will understand very shortly," was the reply, "when they set fire to the house!"

Weena gave a little scream.

"Set fire to the house! What on earth can you be talking about?"

"I have brought you here not only to save you," he answered her, "but to convince you that after tonight we will have no home as it will be burnt to the ground."

"But Papa – " she began. "Papa will be burnt too."

"He will know nothing. I gave him a pill before I left that will make him unconscious for twenty-four hours. By that time he will be buried in his own house which I actually believe he would prefer to being buried anywhere else."

His sister was staring at him incredulously as if she thought it impossible to understand what he was saying.

Because Ivor knew just what she was feeling, he rose and moved closer to her.

"Now listen, Weena," he said, "I have not worried you with this before, but I have known for some time that things were becoming increasingly uncomfortable for us in the neighbourhood."

He paused for a moment before he continued,

"They hate Papa as they hate all those who are in a position of authority and privilege."

"I don't understand what you are saying," Weena wailed.

"Well, to put it very bluntly," Ivor told her, "we are going to have a Revolution all over Russia, not all at once, but slowly until eventually it disposes of the Czar and all those who toady to him."

"I think you must be mad!" Weena gasped. "How can that possibly happen in a country as huge as Russia?"

"There have been Revolutions happening all over," Ivor replied, "and because I realise that our people feel the same I have recently been seeing a girl whose family is one of them, so to speak. Because she was intimate with me, she told me the full truth."

"That they intend to kill our beloved Papa?" Weena said incredulously. "I just don't believe it!"

"You are now going to see it happen and because I did not want you to be distressed or to do anything foolish like pleading with these people, which would have been useless, I have brought you here."

"I cannot believe – you are telling me – the truth," Weena muttered, stumbling over the words.

At the same time she was still looking down at their house below.

She could see that the flaming torches had reached the end of the drive and she realised her brother was right in saying that they were going to burn down her home.

For a moment the mob came to a halt.

Then they started moving towards the house so that one group of the torches went to the North of it while the other went to the South.

It was then that Weena gave a cry.

"Oh, Ivor, Ivor – you must stop them!"

"No one can do that," he said quietly. "In fact there is no one we can turn to for help, who could come in time to save us."

"But if you knew about it," Weena protested, "you could have told someone in the Police or in the Army who would have made those revolutionaries, whoever they are, behave."

Her brother gave a little laugh that had no humour in it.

"No one could do that!" he ejaculated, "just as no one will be able to stop these people from rebelling all over Russia."

He sighed before he went on,

"We are at the edge of the country so that no one will worry unduly when they find out that our home is burnt to the ground and Papa is dead."

Weena gave a little sob, but he continued,

"That is why you and I have to go away now to a new country and that is *England*."

He realised that he was speaking almost to himself.

His sister was mesmerised by the growing flames below.

Now she saw that, after standing for a moment so that the first man waited for the last, someone must have given an order and the mob rushed forward.

The burning torches burst through the windows of the drawing room.

Some of them flared up inside the building and then more were lit to follow those that had gone in first.

It was an agony that she could not even express to realise that the hall was now alight and the kitchen quarters were beginning to blaze.

Then the fire was bursting out in the dining room, the sitting room, the two drawing rooms and eventually, and she could not bear to look at it, the library was burning as well.

How could they do it?

"Now they will burn Papa," she cried frantically.

The words seemed to break from her lips as if she could not prevent herself from uttering them.

She hid her face against her brother's shoulder.

"He will know nothing and feel nothing," he tried to comfort her. "I promise you that he was completely unconscious before I left him. You know, as well as I do, I would not want him to suffer in any way."

"I know that," Weena sobbed. "But it's our lovely ancestral home and now we have nothing."

Her brother's arms tightened round her.

"We only have what I had the foresight to hide away," he replied, "which will, I sincerely believe, at least keep us alive for some time."

There was silence for a moment.

Then Weena asked,

"Is that why you made me give you all Mother's jewellery?"

"I put it in a safe place, where we can collect it. There are also all the clothes you gave me last week which were, I hope, your best."

"They were, because you had told me that we were going to stay with one of your friends," Weena murmured, "who was planning to give a ball for us."

5

"I had no wish to tell you why I wanted them, yet now we own only those dresses and what we now stand up in."

"How could you possibly let them burn everything we owned and which we are so proud of?" Weena asked.

She was thinking of all the pictures that her mother had loved and the furniture that her father had always been so thrilled to have collected throughout his life.

Even as she spoke, the flames leapt through to the top of the house and the roof began to crumble until it was no longer visible.

Now in the light from the fire they could see men moving about below them throwing one torch after another into what was left of the house.

She realised now that her father's bedroom where he was lying had completely disappeared.

She wanted to hide her face against her brother's shoulder and not look at the unfolding tragedy anymore.

Yet it was impossible not to do so.

The fire was getting stronger and stronger and the flames were leaping higher and higher.

Now she could see people running from the village towards it.

There would be no chance of them being able to save it, even if they had wanted to help.

But she had the feeling when her brother told her that they were all rejoicing, they would no longer have to obey the orders given by her father who employed a large number of them.

Perhaps they had hated him as revolutionaries hated anyone they thought was socially above them and made them feel inferior.

She must have trembled because her brother's arms tightened further around her.

"You have to be brave, Weena," he said. "We have to find a new life for ourselves, a new way of living. As I have thought it all out, I will tell you about it as soon as we reach the ship that will carry us to safety."

Weena looked round at the burning house.

"It's a long way – to the sea," she managed to sob.

"I know that!" her brother answered. "That is why two horses are waiting for us in a place where no one will see them. I brought them there this morning and left them enough food and water so that they will carry us safely to where we will escape from Russia. Never, I hope, to come back!"

He spoke with a bitterness in his voice that had not been there before.

Then Weena asked in a quavering voice,

"You really mean that we have now lost everything that was ours?"

"Not quite everything. "But our possessions, our land, our home and, as far as we are both concerned, there will never be a chance of us coming back here to claim our birthright."

"You mean – we are exiled?" Weena asked slowly.

"We are indeed exiled and a large number of people would envy us because we have been well prepared for the inevitable."

He rose to his feet as he was speaking and pulled her to him.

Then, holding her hand, he began to take her down the mountain on the far side.

They had not gone far before she realised that they were out of sight of the house.

But she knew by now that there would be little left except for the fire that would burn perhaps for a day or so before it finally died out.

Weena wanted to cry because it was her home.

She had been so happy there all her life with her father and mother.

She had really believed that all the servants who had served them for so long were their friends and not only respected but loved them.

'I really cannot believe that Nanny,' she wanted to say, 'was one of the people who set fire to our house.'

Yet she was not certain.

There had been rumours for quite some time that the people in the village were discontented.

There had been a bad harvest last year, but it was not only that which was disturbing.

There were stories in all the newspapers and letters from their friends reporting that there was discontent over the whole country.

The Czar was unpopular and so were the rules and regulations by which the country was run.

Weena remembered now that when people came to stay with them, they had horrific stories to tell of people being murdered.

And of those in the Government being attacked in the newspapers and booed in the streets.

There was indeed a vast amount of disaffection in whichever direction they looked.

Weena had not attended to these stories very much.

But she realised when her brother came home that he was continually going into the village as if he found it more interesting than being at home with her.

She was not at all surprised because she knew that he must find it very dull at the house.

At the same time she was aware, because she loved him, that he was worried about something although he did not confide in her as to what it was.

Now she understood.

He must have been aware that they were planning in the village to destroy her father and his family because they owned so much land and in their eyes were therefore grotesquely rich and privileged.

Many of those working for him relied on them for their very existence.

It was not only the servants in the house but those who worked on the farms and the many thousands of acres of agricultural land that made up the family estate.

When her mother died, Weena knew that she was a grievous loss to her father that he was not strong enough to withstand.

A year after her mother was buried, he was taken ill and nothing the doctors could do seemed to make him any better.

He had appointed several managers for the estate who Weena thought were unnecessarily harsh with the men who worked there.

It was whispered in the house amongst the servants that they wanted her father to get well so that they were not bullied and ill-treated, as they were being in his absence, by these new foremen.

Her brother, Ivor, who was three years older than she was, was constantly abroad travelling from country to country and he sent her postcards and letters from most of the places where he stayed.

He had also been to England which he had always wanted to visit because their mother was English.

It was a country that Ivor and Weena had been told about so often and which they admired ever since they had been in the nursery.

"*I wish I could stay longer*," Ivor had written to her when he was last in England, "*but I have been planning to visit Africa and I don't want to alter my plans. At the same time I will come back one day and you must come with me to this gracious country.*"

She wondered where he was taking her now.

But it was impossible to ask him anything further while they were climbing down the mountain.

Then Ivor hurried her to a rough shelter built under some trees, where she saw the horses he had told her about were waiting.

He patted them and talked to them so that they were not restless or upset when he arrived and Weena saw that he had been right when he said that he had fed them and there was plenty of water if they wanted a drink.

Without speaking he lifted her onto the horse which had a side-saddle on it and mounted the other one himself.

Only when they were riding away down the rough road that she knew led to the Black Sea, did she ask him without slowing her speed,

"Where are we going now, Ivor?"

"We are leaving Russia," he said, "as I have told you. The sooner we find the ship, which should be in the harbour, the better I will be pleased."

As he spoke, he looked over his shoulder as if he was afraid that someone might be following them.

For the first time Weena thought that if they were followed it could be someone who wanted to destroy them because they were their father's children.

"Could they really hurt us, Ivor?" she asked, but was instantly afraid of the answer.

He did not speak and they rode on still further until at last she could see the buildings that were warehouses at the end of the harbour.

It seemed extraordinary to her that they should now be leaving Russia with almost what she stood up in and no possessions except the two horses they were riding.

Then she remembered how strange Ivor had been for this last month or two.

Their father had been so ill that he could do nothing and said little when they spoke to him.

And now she understood why Ivor had taken over everything. He was in control of the house and the estate.

Twice he had left to go to one of the large towns that was situated some distance from them.

She knew that, when he was there, he had consulted the local Bank Manager from whom she received cheques to enable her to pay the wages in her brother's absence at the end of each month.

When there had been any money coming in from the sales of the estate's produce, she had handed it over to Ivor and she had always supposed that he had paid it into the bank that her father had used.

Now she remembered that for the last six months he had often gone away at the end of the month and recently he had not given her an address or told her where he was going.

She had always admired her brother because he was very intelligent and her mother had been particularly proud of him.

"Ivor ought to have been in Parliament," she had said more than once to her father.

He knew that she had been thinking of the English Parliament and not the Russian one which was continually being criticised.

Her mother was completely English and her family was well known and highly regarded according to her and many of her relations had been amongst the aristocracy.

She had fallen in love with her husband when he had come to England to stay at the Embassy in London, as one of his close relatives was the Russian Ambassador at the Court of St. James's.

Because her father was tall, very good-looking and had an irresistible charm for women, her mother, who was only just eighteen at the time, had fallen madly in love with him almost as soon as they had met.

He had the chance of marrying quite a number of women because he was so handsome.

But he was, in fact, not like an ordinary Russian.

Those who lived in the South of the country were rather short and found it difficult to be friendly. They were, amongst the haughty Social hostesses, considered not to be appropriate friends for the *debutantes*.

Her father had been the exception.

Because he came from the South of Russia, he was entirely different in looks and, of course, in character from those in the North.

He had travelled extensively as a boy because his father moved constantly from Embassy to Embassy.

He therefore looked unusual for a Russian and did not think like one.

"I suppose," he said once to his children, "I am a Cosmopolitan."

And that had been the truth.

Yet, when he had inherited from his father the huge estate in the Caucasus, he had given up the life he enjoyed moving from country to country and had settled down.

He was content to do so as he was so in love with his wife.

She was not one of the great Social beauties, but they had met unexpectedly at a very grand party given by a fashionable lady who always made it her duty to be nice to foreigners.

"The real trouble with the English," she observed to her husband, "is that they label all foreigners as if they are strange animals living overseas who one need only stare at and not become too familiar with!"

She gave a little giggle.

"I like foreigners, they amuse me. They interest me and they are indeed a refreshing change from the English who think themselves too perfect to be altered in any way."

Weena could remember her mother telling her this and they had both laughed.

"She said it to me," her mother told her, "before I went to the party where I met your father. I knew at once that he was the only man who had ever made my heart beat quicker. In fact I fell in love with him as soon as I saw him."

"And he fell in love with you, Mama," Weena said, who had heard the story many times before.

"He said, as soon as he saw me, he knew that was what he had been seeking all the time he had been going around the world," her mother had replied.

She looked thoughtful as she continued,

"We were married and, as he had no wish to travel any more after his father died, we returned here and settled down, as you might say, to a happiness that I just cannot put into words."

'It was so true,' Weena thought. 'There has never been a couple so attached to each other as my father and mother.'

Her love seemed to shine brilliantly from her and it made everyone round her feel as if they were part of it too.

'Ivor and I were brought up in love,' Weena mused. 'How could we possibly be hated by those round us so that they are prepared to burn my beloved Papa to death?'

She had the distinct feeling that, if her mother had been alive, they would never have touched her, because she meant too much to them.

Her father, however, had grown more Russian as the years passed.

He expected to be obeyed without any argument and without anyone refusing whatever it was he wanted or contradicting him in any way.

'Now,' Weena thought as they rode on, 'we have no home and perhaps like Papa we will have to travel from country to country before we find happiness.'

Her father had spoken so often of the places he had been to and of the beautiful women he had met in France, Italy, Egypt, Australia and many other places.

He always ended his story with how he had seen their mother walk into the room at Lady Cromwell's house in London.

And how he had known the moment he saw her that she had been the woman he had been searching for all the years he had travelled so extensively.

It was a wonderful story and a happy one.

Yet Weena felt that it was dreadfully wrong that her father should be buried by a huge mountain of flames and not lying beside her mother in the churchyard where most of his illustrious ancestors were buried.

Weena had been strictly brought up by her mother as a Christian and so she believed that, while their bodies were left on earth, their souls were together in Heaven.

'If it is true,' she thought as she rode on, 'then they will be looking after Ivor and me when we have nowhere to go and are wanderers in a world where no one wants us.'

"Here we are!" Ivor exclaimed suddenly.

Weena forgot all that she was thinking and looked ahead.

She could see the outline of roofs of buildings at the far end of the harbour.

"I hope that there will be something to eat," Weena said, "because I am feeling really hungry."

Ivor smiled.

"We will have breakfast soon and, if there is no ship in Port, then I am sure I will find something for us."

Weena thought that this was somehow doubtful but she did not argue.

They rode on together in silence until they reached the harbour.

There were two ships docked at the quay and Ivor glanced at them before he said,

"I will show you where we will leave the horses. Someone has already promised me that they will look after them properly for us. They have served us well."

"It has certainly been a pleasure to ride this one," Weena answered. "I only wish that we were not going away."

"There is no question about it," Ivor asserted. "We have to go."

He did not say more.

When they arrived at the harbour, he dismounted and Weena did the same.

He led the way and Weena followed him to where there was a stable for travellers, who only sailed out for the day, to leave their horses until they returned.

Fortunately the stable was completely empty except for one ancient horse, which turned to stare at them as they entered the building.

Ivor tied up his horse and saw that there was food in the manger and water for him and Weena did the same.

Then she followed her brother out of the building and across to the ship.

"I suggest that you wait here," he said, "while I go and see if there is accommodation for us."

There was a convenient seat not far from the ship and Weena sat down on it.

Her brother was away for a short while and then he came back to say,

"This ship is leaving for Constantinople and then it is going on to Athens. I will just find out the destination of the other ship, which does not look so good. Then we can decide which one to board."

He did as he said and came back to tell her,

"That second ship is not good enough for us. Let me take you aboard the first one and put you in your cabin while I go to fetch the luggage we are taking with us."

Because Weena was now feeling tired and a little depressed, she said nothing and her brother led the way.

He climbed aboard and told her to wait while he found someone who would take them to their cabins.

The man spoke a strange language that Weena did not know, but Ivor managed to converse with him and she was shown into quite a comfortable cabin.

It was clean and there was room, she thought, for her trunk that her brother promised to bring her.

He left her there and, although she lay down on the bunk, she did not undress as she did not have a nightgown.

Now she understood why her brother had told her to pack everything that was essential.

He had said that they were going to stay with some friends of his who were very rich and influential.

He was lying to her, but it had made her, as he had intended, pack all her prettiest dresses and everything she would want if she was to stay away for several weeks.

Ivor came back eventually with a man helping him carry her trunks which they set down in the cabin.

Then they went back to fetch his cases which were put in the cabin next door.

Although Weena was tired, she still wanted to talk to Ivor.

She only took off the dress she was wearing when he had taken her up the hill and put on her dressing gown she found almost on the top of one of her trunks.

Then at last there was the sound of them moving into the next cabin and she heard the man thanking her brother profusely for what he had tipped him.

She put her head round the door.

"Come and talk to me, Ivor," she urged. "I must know where we are going and what is happening."

"I think you would be wise to sleep," he replied. "Quite frankly I am very tired myself."

"All right, Ivor," she answered. "But I would like to know if we are going North or South, to the moon or to Hell itself!"

She sighed before she added,

"But I suppose that I must remain in ignorance until tomorrow morning."

Ivor laughed and kissed her.

"Goodnight, Weena. It is more important for you to look really beautiful than to fill your head with a lot of rubbish. I will tell you the truth tomorrow when I hope we will be out to sea. In fact, according to the man who has been helping me, we leave at dawn and that will be very soon."

Weena thought if this was true then he was right in saying that they should have plenty of sleep before the ship set out to sea.

Wherever they were going, it did not really matter as long as they were not left behind to be treated as her poor father had been.

'How could they do that to my Papa?' she asked herself over and over again.

Somehow she thought that, however bad the feeling was against the authorities in St. Petersburg, no one would care what happened in the Caucasus.

Yet now as she thought about it she knew that there had been many fiery speeches locally from those who had declared themselves against the Government.

There had also been a great deal of discontent even amongst those who worked for her father and it was as if, for the last few years, everyone in the whole country was dissatisfied with Russia as it was.

Although they did not come so far South, she knew that there were people who already had a big following trying to change the laws and attacking the autocratic Czar.

Yet whatever they said, however intimidating, they avoided any punishment.

She had not really followed events very closely as she had been so busy at home.

It was only when her brother was there to translate what was being said into plain language, so that she could understand it, that she had been worried that it might affect the quietness of their own village and their own people.

'Surely the rest of the country is fairly prosperous,' she reflected. 'Why should they always be railing against those in authority?'

There was no one to answer her questions and in time she ceased to ask them.

She had busied herself in caring for her sick father who saw innumerable doctors and specialists without there being any improvement in his health.

She did her best to keep the garden as beautiful as her mother had always wanted it to be, and every week she had taken some of the flowers down to the little churchyard where her mother was buried and put them on her tomb.

Then she had gone into the Church to pray that her mother would look after her and make her father better.

She thought that if she lost him she would be losing almost her whole family.

Then to her great relief Ivor had come back home and everything had changed.

She was not alone, he was with her.

He explained to her all the problems she had had no answer to in the past.

Now, when she least expected it, the revolutionaries had attacked her father and he was no longer there.

She and Ivor were setting off on some wild strange adventure and she had no idea what the end would be.

'It is all very frightening,' she thought. 'So please Papa and Mama, if you are together think of us and please help us.'

It was a prayer that came from her heart which she felt flew up to Heaven.

'I know that they will be thinking of us,' she told herself before she fell sleep.

CHAPTER TWO

When Weena woke in the morning, it was because there was a noise coming from the cabin next door.

Listening very closely, she could hear her brother's voice ringing out and she was certain that he was giving orders.

It seemed very strange that he was doing so on the ship, but still there was this noise in the cabin next to hers.

Obviously the walls between her cabin and the next one were not very thick.

Because she had no idea of the time, except that it was daylight and the sun was shining, she wondered if she should get up now or wait for her brother to tell her what was happening.

Suddenly the noise ceased.

Then there was the sound of more voices, but she could not understand what they were saying.

Finally, at the moment when she felt that she must at last get out of bed, the door opened and Ivor put his head round.

"Are you awake?" he asked.

"I was woken by all that noise next door," Weena replied, "and I could not think what it was."

He gave a laugh and came into her cabin, closing the door behind him.

"Actually the noise was everything we possess and we have to make it last for a long time."

Weena did not know what he was talking about.

She sat up in bed and stared at him before she said,

"I don't know what you mean, but I am extremely curious."

"When you are dressed," Ivor replied, sitting down on the bed, "you will find that the next cabin is filled with trunks and cases all containing, as I have already told you, everything we now possess."

Weena stared at him.

The sun, streaming through the porthole, turned her hair to gold.

She looked as if she was an angel with the light of Heaven behind her.

"You are very pretty," Ivor said unexpectedly, as if he was speaking to himself. "That will be tremendously helpful to us both in London."

Weena drew in her breath.

"Is that really where we are going?"

"We are travelling to England," Ivor replied, "and we are now going to forget what happened last night and actually, for the moment, Russia as a whole."

Weena did not try to ask him why, although she did not understand.

She only sat looking at him wide-eyed.

"Let me start at the beginning," Ivor said, "and tell you that I have realised for quite a long time that this was about to happen. So I have taken every possible precaution I could to see that you and I don't starve to death."

"Thank goodness!" she exclaimed. "But then you have always been very clever and I feel sure that you will prevent us both from dying of anything quite as horrible as starvation."

"That is exactly what I intend to do," Ivor replied. "So you will find next door that there are not only your clothes and mine but everything I could manage to take out of the house without anyone being suspicious."

Weena gave a little gasp.

"Out of the house?" she quizzed.

"When I guessed that this was about to happen, as I told you, I made a friend of one of the girls in the village who was pretty and rather better bred than most of them. Because she loved me, she told me all the secrets that were being whispered at that time behind closed doors."

"Secrets about what?"

"About taking over Father's estate for one thing," Ivor replied, "and also about the beginning of a Revolution in almost every part of our country."

"Can that really be true?" Weena asked him in a frightened voice.

"I am afraid it is. When the revolutionaries finally get their own way, they will dispose of the Czar and run the country as they think it ought to be run and that will be definitely not be as it is now."

"How could they do anything so wicked?" Weena asked. "Besides Russia is so enormous, they could never have revolutionaries all over such a great area."

"That unfortunately is what many people at the top think, but then I have studied this very carefully and I can promise you, my dear Weena, that these revolutionaries are creeping in everywhere. Sooner or later they will gain the control they are determined to acquire by any means."

There was silence for a moment.

Then Weena asked in a trembling voice,

"What will happen to us?"

"That is exactly what I am going to tell you," Ivor said. "I am only so thankful and very grateful to Fate that I realised in time how serious the situation had become in our country."

"But you could not save Papa – " she whispered.

"As you well know, Papa has been suffering from the stroke that the doctors had no cure for. As they told me frankly, he was bound to die sooner rather than later."

Ivor stopped for a moment as if he found it difficult to say more and then he added very quietly,

"I think, rather than realise that he was a prisoner and his lands were being taken away from him, he would have wanted to die. As it is, he will not have suffered in any way."

"Now *we* are suffering," Weena murmured. "We have lost Papa, our home, our land, in fact everything we loved and which meant so much to Mama."

There was silence.

Then Ivor said,

"You may think it imagination, but I felt last night, as I have felt before, that Mama is guiding us. The one thing that she wanted more than anything else was that you should be taken to safety."

Weena wiped away the tears that had come into her eyes and then she asked again,

"How are we going to live? There is nowhere for us to go."

She was thinking that there were no relations they could turn to for help.

Their grandfather had broken away from his family to build a house in the Caucasus and become a large and respected landowner.

When their father had inherited the estate, he had carried on his father's work of buying and developing more and more land.

He was not ambitious socially in any way. He was quite content with the rural life in the beautiful Caucasus.

But he could have gained a number of honours and doubtless if he had tried hard he could have found, as most Russians had found, that there was a title somewhere in his extensive family.

"Papa always claimed that he had no wish to be a Socialite," Weena said when her brother told her this.

"I well remember him saying it," Ivor replied. "But things are very different where we are concerned."

She wondered what he meant.

Then he expanded,

"When I knew how difficult it was going to be for us in the future if anything happened to Papa and I learnt from my friend in the village what those subversives were planning, I started to move objects of value from the house which we will now be very thankful to take with us."

"Is that what you were busy moving into the next cabin?" she enquired.

"Exactly," her brother answered. "You will be very surprised to see how clever I have been."

"I don't understand what we are taking with us," Weena said.

"Well, first of all I have brought quite a number of Papa's best pictures. I know they are valuable and that I will be able to sell them in London for quite a considerable sum."

"The pictures!" Weena cried. "But they are huge!"

Her brother laughed.

"I have taken them out of their frames and rolled up the canvases and they are packed, securely I would hope. But I am not at all surprised when they carried them into next door that they woke you up."

"Pictures!" she exclaimed again. "I certainly did not think of you taking away the pictures."

"I took Papa's valuable collection of miniatures and his snuff boxes as well," Ivor told her.

Weena gave a little cry of delight.

"Oh, I am so glad you saved those. I love them and I could not bear them to have been burnt to ashes in that terrible fire."

"Which they would have been with everything else we possessed."

There was a harsh note in Ivor's voice.

She knew by the way he spoke that he was minding as much as she did that the house, which had been their home and made so glorious by their mother and father, was now burnt to the ground.

"You said," Weena reiterated after a long silence, "that you could get a good price for the pictures in London. So that is where we are definitely going?"

"Yes, that is where we are going," Ivor answered. "But we have to be sensible and realise that what we have brought with us, even though it may fetch a certain amount of money, will not be enough to keep us for the rest of our lives."

"No, of course not," Weena agreed, "but perhaps we can find some paid work to do."

As she spoke, she was wondering just what sort of work she was capable of doing and whether it would be available to her even if she could find it.

She had been brought up, now she thought about it, to enjoy herself and to ride her father's excellent horses

25

and to help her mother grow the flowers in the garden that meant so much to them both and to read the books in the library that she loved so intensely.

She was wise enough to realise that none of these activities of hers were saleable.

And, although she was sure that Ivor would be able to find something interesting he could exert himself in, she could think of nothing that anyone would pay her to do.

As if he knew exactly what she was thinking, Ivor suggested,

"Forget that nonsense. If you think I am going to have you obeying the orders of other people or even being a companion to some elderly person so that you could have your board and lodging free, you are mistaken."

"I was actually thinking how helpless I am and how little I am able to do," Weena replied forlornly.

"You are very beautiful, very intelligent and I am quite certain that there are a great number of men who will find you irresistible."

Weena stared at him.

"Are you saying that I must get married?"

"Of course you must," Ivor replied, "and to the first important, distinguished and rich gentleman who loses his heart to you."

Weena drew in her breath.

"But we don't know anyone like that in England."

She paused for a moment before she went on,

"Even if we did, I would not want to marry anyone unless I loved him like Papa and Mama loved each other."

"That is what we all want," Ivor said harshly. "But we have to be practical and to keep alive you have to find a rich husband and I have to find a rich wife."

"Do you really mean that?" Weena asked him.

"Of course I mean it. Anyway, as you are so pretty, you will undoubtedly have quite a number of men wanting to marry you."

"But how will I meet them? You know as well as I do that we know no one in England. Mama often said that everyone she knew well had died and she had no wish to go back to England because she would be a stranger in her own country."

"Mama would have found quite a number of people who would have welcomed her with open arms," Ivor told her. "And she would have found that she still had a few relations left even if they did live in the North of England rather than in London."

"I am sure they are all dead by now," Weena said.

"I expect they are," Ivor agreed. "But we are not looking for relatives. We will be going as ourselves and as ourselves we *will* be a success."

He spoke so positively that Weena could only say hesitatingly,

"How can you be sure – of that?"

"Because the English are snobs," he answered her. "We will both have what they expect of every important Russian – *a title*."

"A title!" Weena exclaimed. "And just how can we possibly acquire one?"

Her brother smiled.

"I rather fancy myself as Prince Ivor Kerlensky and you, my dear, will be a Princess."

"You must be joking," Weena said incredulously. "How could we possibly be that when you know as well as I do that there were very few titles in the Caucasus and any Russians, if we meet them, would know at once that we are imposters."

"That is where you are wrong, dear sister. I have gone into this matter most carefully and I have discovered that there are hundreds and hundreds of Princes in Russia because, as you know, every member of a major family has a title."

He smiled at her before he continued,

"If one's father and mother are Prince and Princess, each child is also a Prince or Princess and the same applies to any children that they may have and so on."

Weena did not speak and he went on,

"In England it is different. They have one big title, like a Duke or an Earl, and only the eldest son inherits it. His son has to wait with an inferior title, if one at all, until his father surrenders his by death."

"I know all that because Mama told me about it," Weena replied. "One of her many relations, an uncle, was a politician and he became a Lord and went to the House of Lords. But unfortunately he had no son."

"I remember Mama talking about him," Ivor said. "She was very proud of her family. But, as I have already discovered, there are more or less none of them left. If there was, they would take little notice of us, as they would feel we were expecting them to help us out of our poverty and then undoubtedly become an encumbrance."

Weena was silent and after a moment he went on,

"But as far as I know there is no family in Russia called Kerlensky and, if there was, they are not likely to come to London to see if we are or are not their relatives."

"Do you really think that we can pretend to be – a Prince and – a Princess?"

Weena spoke in a way that told him without words, that she thought it was not only impossible but something that they should not do as it was morally wrong.

"Now listen to me, Weena," he said. "We have just seen our home burnt before our very eyes. We know that the land will now be taken over by revolutionaries and we have no possible way of making them give it back to us. We, therefore, have to make a new life for ourselves in a new country and be very brave about it."

He turned towards her as he added,

"But, Weena, we are not so stupid as to arrive as two unimportant youngsters who, in Social London, would undoubtedly be ignored by everyone of any standing."

"And you really think that – if we arrive as Prince and Princess they will then at least invite us to one meal?"

"I hope they will do a great deal more than that," Ivor replied. "I am not as foolish as you obviously think I am."

"No, no, that's not true, I have always thought you wonderful, Ivor and, of course, very handsome. I am sure, if they really believe that you are a Prince, you will look exactly as a Prince should do."

She waited and, as her brother did not answer, she went on,

"But I don't think that 'Princess Weena' will invite much interest."

"You are quite right in thinking that Weena is not particularly impressive," he replied. "But as Mama always called you that I have really forgotten the numerous names you were baptised with."

"I suppose," Weena said when he paused, "I could call myself by one of the other names that I was christened with. Equally I am quite certain I will never remember to answer to it."

She was thinking of how her name had never been a real one but a word of love.

She had been born prematurely and her mother had often told her how she looked so small and so sweet that she had almost cried with delight when they put her into her arms.

"You were no bigger than the doll I had loved when I was a child," her mother had told her. "I exclaimed how weeny you were. 'My weeny baby,' I said over and over again until everyone laughed and declared when they gave you to me, 'here is your weeny baby and be very careful, as she is so small, that you don't crush her'."

"So that is the reason I am called 'Weena'," she had answered.

Her mother had then told her.

"Even after we christened you, I kept calling you 'Weena' because you were so sweet and so small. It was Papa who said that we would call you 'Weena' because it is easier to remember than any of the names you had been christened with."

So 'Weena' had come into being.

She thought now that it would be very difficult to remember that her other names were Sofiate and Nadjavat.

"Of course I do realise that you will not want those names," Ivor said before she could speak again. "So I have found a name for you that I know you will appreciate. You will be Princess Alweena Kerlensky which you must admit sounds very impressive."

Weena stared at him.

Then suddenly she clapped her hands together.

"I like it! I do like it!" she exclaimed. "I should hate to have to give up completely the name that our Mama always called me."

"Of course you would," Ivor agreed, "that is why I have planned it all very carefully. As Princess Alweena, I promise you, you will be a huge success in London."

"I only hope you are right," Weena replied a little doubtfully.

At the same time, although she did not say so, she could not bear to think of marrying a man just because he was rich and important. Not, as she had always meant it to be, because she loved him.

Her mother had told her so often how she and her father had fallen in love from the very first moment they had looked into each other's eyes.

And how happy she had been even though she had to live in a foreign country where she knew no one.

"If I am to be truthful I wanted no one except your father," she had said. "We always do everything together, absolutely everything, and we want our two lovely children to be as happy as we are."

Weena could understand when her mother died how her father seemed suddenly to age overnight.

He was lost without her and, although Weena tried in every way to make him happy, it was difficult for him even to pretend that he was not desperately lonely without the wife he had loved so passionately for over thirty years.

Now he was dead as well and Weena was left with only Ivor.

If he married, she would be alone in a hostile world she knew nothing about.

As if he was following his own thoughts, Ivor went on,

"You may think that I am asking too much of life, but I took the precaution in case this happened. I have been bright enough to study the English newspapers wherever I went and whenever I could find them."

He chuckled as he continued,

"I have made a list of people who had entertained a Russian grandee, who I gather was a great success with the elite of London who cluster round the Prince of Wales."

"Who was that?" Weena asked him.

"I don't suppose you would know who I mean," Ivor replied, "even though I have talked about him to you on various occasions. His name is Prince Feodor Sazanov. He is related to the Czar and is of great consequence in St. Petersburg."

He paused before he added,

"I gather from what I read that, when he went to England, he was accepted not only by the Prince of Wales but also by Queen Victoria, who gave a party for him at Windsor. All the time he was last in England he appeared in the Social columns of one hostess or another and I made a list of them."

His sister stared at him.

"How will that help us?" she asked.

Her brother smiled.

"Because I once met Prince Feodor when I was in St. Petersburg and I thought him very charming. He was very kind to me although I was of no great standing."

"How does that help us?" Weena asked impatiently.

"Because, my dear sister, he died around a month or so ago and was deeply mourned in many parts of Russia. I am sure that there are a number of people in London who will feel the same when hear about his death."

Weena was listening.

At the same time she was wondering how all this could possibly concern them.

"What I intend to do," Ivor continued, "is to write to a number of the friends who entertained Prince Feodor when he was in England saying he had told me that if I ever visited London he would give me an introduction to them, but that he has unfortunately died."

"He is dead, so how can he possibly help us now?"

"I will tell them that I am missing him dreadfully as I am sure that they must be too," Ivor replied. "But I am certain that he would want me to tell his friends how fond he was of them and how he had told me of their kindness and gracious hospitality when he was visiting London."

Weena was listening intently, but she still found it hard to believe how this could really help them.

As if he realised what she was thinking, her brother said,

"Don't be silly! If they were so devoted to Prince Feodor as they appear to have been, they would have to ask us at least once to dine with them or even just call on them at their London homes."

Weena gave a gasp.

"So that is how you intend to get to know them!"

"You must admit that it's a good plan," her brother replied. "One Russian is certainly as good as another and who knows they may take a fancy to me so that you and I are persona grata at their parties."

"Oh, Ivor, I do think you are clever," Weena said. "I can only pray that all your planning will come off."

"Well, now I think you should get up," Ivor said, "while I go and take some air. Then I will show you the extent of our hidden hoard of treasure in the next cabin."

He left her cabin as he spoke.

As Weena heard him going along the passage, she thought that she must be dreaming.

Exactly how could this all have happened to her so quickly?

Ivor's plans seemed to her to be so extraordinary and almost like a story in a book she had read.

'Just how can we possibly pretend to be Prince and Princess?' she asked herself. 'What will happen if anyone exposes us?'

She knew that Ivor was right in saying that there were thousands of Princes and Princesses in Russia and so no one would be surprised in the slightest at meeting them.

In fact, they would be even more surprised if they did not possess a title to flaunt in front of London Society.

'I hope and pray that we will not be exposed,' she thought as she dressed. 'At the same time I do see that, if we are to be a success in London, people will expect us to be titled and be of no interest whatsoever if we are not.'

She was fastening her dress with more than a little difficulty when Ivor came back.

He saw at once what she was doing and buttoned up the back of her dress with an expertise that told her that he had doubtless had plenty of practice with the beautiful women he had encountered since he grew up.

"Now come on and see what I have brought with us," he suggested. "I would like to point out that I have been taking items to the harbour at night as it would be a mistake for anyone locally to realise what I was doing."

"You are very ingenious to think of such a brilliant idea," Weena replied. "However, I know it would be very strange to think of us as people of great importance rather than two unknown country bumpkins."

"That is something you will never be, because you are too beautiful," her brother answered. "You have to admit that Mama was never anything but a graceful and very beautiful Lady whatever name she might have called herself."

"Of course you are right in that," Weena agreed. "I will try to be like Mama whom everyone admired from the lowest of those working for us right up to the aristocrats we sometimes entertained."

"Which was not often, as Papa found them a bore. Although she seldom talked about it, Mama was a great success when they travelled to St. Petersburg just after they were married."

He paused before he carried on,

"There was no doubt that the Czar and the Czarina found her charming. They were well aware that she came from a most distinguished English family."

"If they were alive now," Weena asked, "I wonder if they would be ashamed of what we are doing or perhaps commend us for being intelligent enough to give it a try."

Ivor chuckled.

"Equally we have to achieve what we desire and that is a charming rich husband for you and an even richer bride for me!"

While Weena was thinking that her mother would have told them to marry for love, she wondered how her brother would be able to put up with a woman when her only attraction was her bank balance.

Undoubtedly the woman would marry him because he was so handsome.

But once they were married he might find another woman far more attractive.

She did not, of course, put these ideas into words, because she felt that Ivor would not appreciate them at this stage of their escape.

He took her by the hand and ushered her a short distance along the corridor to another cabin.

Weena looked inside this cabin, which was a little larger than hers, with sheer astonishment.

It seemed to be filled with trunks and cases, some of which she recognised as having been up in the attics at home for many years.

Some she could see were new and Ivor must have purchased them for this very purpose.

"Let me explain to you," he began, "what I have in each one of these. Of course, the two trunks in which you packed everything you needed will save us from spending too much money on decorating you as a beautiful Russian Princess until we can afford all the fashionable clothes you will need when you are established as one of the beauties of London."

Weena gave a cry.

"Oh, do be careful, Ivor. You are asking too much of me. How can I possibly compete with women who will undoubtedly be even more beautiful than our Mama? They will look on me as an interloper and a foreigner."

She paused and, as he did not speak, she went on,

"You know just as well as I do that the English are always supposed to heartily dislike foreigners and consider themselves superior to any other race."

"They may do that *en masse*," her brother replied, "but when it comes down to rank I can assure you that the English, as a whole, are very impressed by titles."

He smiled at her before he continued,

"I expect it's because they are very mean with their own. A Prince and Princess in England are rare and rather glamorous. While in Russia, as we all know, a Prince is of little standing unless he lives in the shadow of the Czar."

"I suppose that's true," she said in a small voice. "Now tell me what else you have taken from our home without my realising it."

There were quite a number of items that she had not expected and yet each of them was of considerable value.

She applauded her brother that he had been clever enough to think that they should have suitable presents to give to those who entertained them.

He had therefore packed in one case a great number of small but pretty objects which had decorated side tables in rooms that were not very often used, but which would be much appreciated by those who received them.

Yet it would cost them nothing.

"I think you have been very, very clever," she said finally when he told her what was in all the trunks. "I am sure the pictures will, as you say, bring in a good sum of money."

"I hope so. But remember, Weena, when this is all spent, there will be nothing left. By that time we must both be married. So what it really amounts to is that there is no time to be lost."

He spoke so positively and with a note of authority in his voice that told his sister he was determined to win this particular battle.

Once again she felt herself shrinking away from the prospect and she really wanted to ask him,

'What about love? What about finding a man who I love for himself and not because he has a large fortune or perhaps a huge estate?"

She realised that Ivor would find such a question extremely stupid.

He would point out in no uncertain terms it was a question of marriage or starvation and that was something neither of them would enjoy.

'It is going to be difficult, I know it's going to be difficult,' she mused.

But she told herself severely that it was something that she must not say aloud.

"So now you see," Ivor was saying, "I have been very astute and we must not allow the English to know for a moment that this is all we own and when it is gone there will be nothing to replace it."

Weena slipped her arm through his.

"I realise that, dearest. You have been very shrewd and I admire you very much. I can only pray that neither of us will be disappointed."

Even as she was speaking to him she felt a sudden shrinking within her heart.

Once again she was feeling afraid that she would never find love, the real love that had made her father and mother so blissfully happy.

*

The ship was now moving through the Black Sea.

When they went up on deck, Weena knew that once they were into the Dardanelles and down into the Sea of Marmara, they would have left Russia for ever.

They were now setting out, as she knew when she gazed at the waves, on a great adventure.

At the same time, although she did not dare say so to Ivor, she was afraid that it would all end up a failure.

If it was, what would happen then?

Where could they go?

Who would help them?

She knew, as she looked at the sea, that they were leaving behind everything that had been hers since she had been born.

They were facing the unknown.

What would the future hold for her?

Would she find happiness?

Would she perhaps know the emptiness and misery of never finding love?

CHAPTER THREE

The sea was fairly calm, but, as Weena had nothing else to do, she went to her cabin after luncheon and lay down.

She had nearly drifted off into a deep sleep, but still worrying about the future, when her brother came into the cabin.

"I thought that you were up on deck," he said, "and have been looking for you."

"I became tired of staring at the sea, so I thought I would lie down and think about myself," Weena replied.

He laughed and sat down on the end of the bed.

"I have been talking to the Captain, who is a very charming man and interested in us. He has given me some excellent advice."

Weena pushed herself up against the pillows.

"What is it?" she asked.

"He told me that if we arrive in Athens and pick up an English ship, if we are not careful we will be charged much too much and waste our precious money."

Weena gave a gasp.

"We must not do that!"

"I am well aware that everything we have with us has to last us a very long time," Ivor said. "Therefore I listened attentively to the Captain when he told me that in the new ships coming from the different countries the First

Class passengers are really ripped off in a most unpleasant way."

"What do you mean by that?" Weena enquired.

"Well, they think if they are rich enough to travel First Class they are rich enough to pay for everything they do. If we arrive saying that we are a Prince and Princess we will, in English parlance, 'be taken to the cleaners'."

Weena laughed.

They had learnt a fair amount of English slang from a maid their mother had employed at one time to look after them and do the odd jobs in the house.

She was a good Cockney and she taught Ivor and Weena who were by that time getting older, some choice Cockney slang that they enjoyed using between themselves and when they were talking to their mother.

Their father disliked them speaking English and so always insisted that they speak the best and most correct Russian to him.

In consequence, of course, they were fascinated by the English Cockney and used it to tease their mother and make her laugh.

"I don't quite understand," Weena said, "why they should want to do that. At the same time, as you say, we have all we possess with us and we must be very careful not to waste any money unnecessarily."

"That is just what I was thinking," Ivor said, "and the first thing we have to do is to change our names. We must not be Russian, as the Captain has warned us against that. They think that the Russians are pretty soft when it comes to taking money off them."

"If then we are to be English," Weena observed, "we must choose a name that does not sound too grand."

"That is exactly what I was thinking," Ivor agreed. "You can therefore have your choice."

"Then let's think of what names there are," Weena answered. "Jones? I remember that was the name of the girl who stayed with us for almost two years."

"She taught us quite a lot," Ivor commented.

"We can easily use her language to tell people just how common we are!" Weena laughed.

"I hope we would never be considered common! And anyway you, my lovely sister, could never in a million years look anything but very pretty."

"While you are tall, handsome and actually look far more English than Russian," Weena told him.

"That is the sort of remark that you would not have dared to say in front of Papa, but I know it's true because the English friends I made said I looked very much like them."

"From what I remember they were rather smart and came from good families, so you could hardly impersonate one of them."

"Of course not," Ivor agreed. "That is why I have been buying items in Russia to sell in England. We want a good name to impress them that we are ordinary English tradespeople. What name do you suggest?"

"Brown?"

"No!"

"Potter?"

"No!"

"Cook?"

"No!"

"Wilkins?"

"Oh, no!" Weena exclaimed. "They sound terrible. I absolutely refuse to have a name like that."

"Then what do you propose?" Ivor asked.

Weena thought for a moment.

Then she said,

"Do you remember Mama saying that she once had a Governess called Dawson? I would say that name is very English and at the same time quite a respectable name."

"You are a genius!" he exclaimed. "Dawson it will be. Ivor Dawson really sounds rather grand. It's a name you could trust not to defraud you."

Weena laughed.

"I am sure that is something you would never do."

"I hope not," he replied. "We are only telling a very small lie in saying that I am a salesman because that is exactly what I am. But the people on this ship must not know how valuable our cargo is."

"I will remember, when we reach Athens, that I am Weena Dawson," his sister said slowly. "I think it's a good idea for us to travel Second Class or at least not in the grand cabins which I believe in the modern ships are very lavish."

"We will have two ordinary cabins," Ivor replied. "If we are not as comfortable as we might be, at least we will be saving our money for England."

Weena wanted to say how much she hoped that he would obtain good prices for his pictures and all the other items they had brought from their home.

But she thought it would be a mistake to make him in any way nervous that what they did possess might not reach the high prices he was hoping for.

Because Ivor was constantly talking to the Captain, Weena found herself wandering on her own about the ship and thinking of the strange new life that lay ahead of them.

She could only pray that things would be as easy as Ivor expected them to be.

Then they would both be accepted in London by the people they wanted to know.

She had heard so much about English Society and how they clustered round the Prince of Wales and his wife and, of course, his glorious mother, Queen Victoria.

Her mother had often talked of the parties and balls she had attended in London when she had been a girl.

Weena had listened attentively, but never thought that she would be able to enjoy the same sort of life.

The Social world in the Caucasus was very small and, when she met the people who were their neighbours, she found them rather dull and they knew very little about anything outside the Caucasus.

Fortunately her beloved father had always been a great reader, thus the extensive library in the house, which had been a sheer delight to Weena from the moment she grew older.

Now when she thought of it burnt to dust and ashes, she wished she had brought with her a number of books even though it would have made the amount of luggage they were travelling with bigger than it was already.

Anyway she was quite certain that Russian books in England were not saleable.

She appreciated the fact that Ivor had been clever enough to take away a great number of objects before the house had burnt down, which were not only valuable but saleable.

*

When they reached Greece, Weena was so excited because she had read so much about the many Greek Gods and Goddesses of Classical times.

She was thrilled at the thought of having a chance to see some of the ancient Temples that had been described in the books she had read.

And she was, in fact, delighted when Ivor told her when they went ashore that there were no English ships in Port at the moment, but several were expected in during the next day or so.

They said their farewells to the friendly Captain, who wished them the best of luck and he told Ivor that he was a very brave man.

"There are not many of you leaving Russia at the moment," he confided. "If you ask me, they will soon be finding things are uncomfortable and will then want to live somewhere else."

"You are quite right," Ivor said. "I can only thank you for all the advice you have given me and I hope that we will meet again.

"I hope that we will too," the Captain replied. "Do make sure you look after that pretty sister of yours and see that she does not get into trouble. The English are famous for running after a pretty woman, but not quite as much as the French!"

The two men laughed at this and Weena, because they were talking about her, felt rather shy.

Their luggage was taken ashore and placed in the safe-keeping of one of the men whose job it was to see that nothing was stolen from where they deposited it.

"Now what I am going to do," Ivor said, "is to walk round the Port to find out all I can about the ships heading for England."

He smiled at his sister.

"The Captain said that they expected two or three in the next day or so, but I want to find out about them and if they are the sort of ship we should travel in to Dover."

"I do want to go while we are in Athens and see some of the Temples and statues I have read about in my books," Weena told him.

Her brother hesitated for a moment.

Then he said,

"Well, if you are sure you can take care of yourself and do not talk to strangers, you should be all right. But don't go too far or be away too long."

"I just want to see what I can of Greece while I am here," Weena persisted. "I have read so much about the beauty of its Temples that still exist that I would feel very ashamed if I did not see them while I am actually standing on Greek soil."

"All right, off you go," Ivor said. "We will meet back here in a couple of hours."

In case he changed his mind, Weena set off at once.

She saw that the houses round the Port were small and rather dilapidated.

But, as she passed them and entered the town, she had her first glimpse of what seemed to her a magnificent Temple.

She realised that there was a lot of broken statues on either side of the road and she so wished that she had someone with her who could tell her about them.

But it was almost enough just to see the beauty of the statues even though many of them needed repairing and were suffering from old age and neglect.

She walked until she saw on one side of her, what she was sure must be the Parthenon.

It was built on high ground so that she had to climb over some very rough rocks to enter it.

It was just as exciting as she expected it to be and she felt that there was a very special atmosphere about the Parthenon.

She had felt the same when she read the books on Greece and she had known that in some strange way they meant a great deal to her, although she could not exactly put it into words.

The tall statues inside the Temple were even more beautiful than those she had seen along the roadside.

She went from one to the other thinking that only ancient Greece had been able to depict a woman in stone and make her as stunningly beautiful as if she was living and breathing.

She was so intent on what she was seeing that it was with a start she realised that time had passed and that she should be returning to the Port where Ivor would be waiting for her.

It was then she noticed that she had walked right through the Parthenon.

When she came out at the other end, there was then a long drop down onto the bare ground beneath it.

She had a feeling that it would take her a long time to find her way back.

The quickest way would be for her to climb down from where she was now and then make for the road that led back to the Port.

The only problem seemed to be the long drop from the building to the ground and there did not appear to be a path unless she went back the way she had come in.

'I am sure I can manage it,' she decided.

Equally it was a long way to fall and she might hurt easily herself.

She sat down at the edge of the Temple and thought perhaps if she let herself down gently, holding tightly onto the stone wall above her, she would then only have to drop down a few feet.

She could then reach what appeared to be much less rocky ground than there had been in front of the building.

But it was definitely a long drop and she felt rather frightened.

It was then unexpectedly from beneath her a voice asked,

"Can I help you?"

She looked down and saw a man gazing up at her.

She realised that he had spoken to her in English.

"I would be very very grateful if you could do so," she answered. "I am frightened of falling and it's such a long way back to the front of the Temple."

He smiled.

"This is definitely the quickest way if you want to return to civilisation. But you will have to trust me not to let you fall."

She then glanced down and thought once again that it was dangerous and that she might hurt herself.

Admittedly there was plenty of grass on the ground below, but there were a number of sharp looking stones as well.

"Just trust me," the man said. "I promise you that you will not hurt yourself."

He stood below her and held out his arms.

She lowered herself as carefully as she could until he was able to clasp her first round the legs and then round her waist.

She reached the ground with the man holding onto her tightly for the last yard.

Then breathlessly she stammered,

"Thank you – very much – it was so kind of you."

"You have to be careful in these ruins," he replied. "The stones round them are very sharp and I have heard that several people have injured themselves considerably by falling on them."

"I can only thank you for saving me," Weena said. "Now, as I am already late, I must hurry back to the ship."

"Why are you leaving Greece in such a hurry?" he asked.

"I only wish we could stay longer," Weena replied, "but my brother and I are travelling to England."

"Then I will not keep you," the stranger said. "But I hope you will have happy memories of Greece rather than injured ones."

"I will indeed – thanks to you," Weena answered.

She smiled at him.

Then, because she knew that Ivor would be angry if she kept him waiting, she started to run towards the road.

When she reached it, she turned back and saw that the stranger who had helped her was standing where she had left him.

She waved her hand and he waved back.

Then she started to run along the road, on which there was very little traffic, towards the Port.

When she arrived there breathlessly, she found, as she expected, that Ivor was waiting impatiently for her.

"You are late," he scolded her. "I began to worry that you might have been captured by brigands or far more likely joined the Gods at Olympus."

"I would love to do that," Weena replied. "Have you found a ship for us, Ivor?"

"There is one coming in later this afternoon from Constantinople and they have assured me that we will have no difficulty in getting aboard it."

"That sounds excellent news," Weena said. "All the same I would like to have stayed longer in Greece."

"We must not waste our money unnecessarily!" he replied sharply. "England is where our future comfort lies and the sooner we get down to business the better."

Weena drew in her breath.

She knew exactly what he was saying.

But she had no wish to be married especially to a man who she would have to marry not for love but because he was rich and influential.

Yet it was no use saying so to Ivor. He had planned everything and for the moment at any rate she must agree with him.

They had something to eat and drink in the nearest café to the Port.

All the time Ivor was watching out to catch sight of the English ship that he had been told about sailing in from Constantinople.

"I am thankful to say," he said, "that they told me it is not one of the largest or most expensive ships which the English now have on the seas. However it is a comfortable one. That will give us a chance to relax and plan what we will do when we reach London."

"It still frightens me to think that we know no one," Weena answered, "and I am still hoping that the people on your list will invite us to their parties."

"They will invite us if they think we are important enough. So you must never forget for a moment that you are a Princess and I am a Prince."

"Are we using these new identities on the ship?" Weena asked.

Ivor shook his head.

"No, of course no! They would expect us to pay far more than I intend to pay for the trip. We only become distinguished when we are actually on British soil. If by any chance they realise that we have been calling ourselves Dawson, it was merely because we had no wish for anyone to treat us as if we were Royalty and so we are travelling incognito."

Weena laughed.

"You have certainly thought out every little detail. I do think it's very intelligent of you. At the same time I admit that I am rather frightened."

"Just leave everything to me, Weena, I have been planning this now for a long time. As I have told you, there will be many people who will, I am certain, be only too pleased to welcome us to their houses because we were such good friends of Prince Feodor."

Weena thought that there was a certain amount of risk in his plan.

But she did not say so.

She merely waited as her brother was doing until the English ship sailed into Port.

They saw that a fair number of those travelling on it were disembarking and they obviously intended to stay in Athens because their luggage was taken off with them.

Ivor waited until the ship seemed empty of those who had been travelling on it before he went on board to visit the Purser.

"My name is Dawson," he then introduced himself. "My sister and I want two cabins that are comfortable, but not too expensive."

The Purser smiled.

"Welcome aboard, sir. I am sure we will be able to accommodate you."

"I hope so," Ivor replied. "I have quite a number of goods from Russia that I am taking back to England to be sold and they are valuable to me. I hope that you will be able to arrange a safe place for them where they will not be damaged or stolen."

"I assure you, sir, nothing is stolen from this ship," the Purser said. "As to your luggage being valuable, we can deposit it in a locked storage room where it will be perfectly safe until we arrive in London."

"That is exactly what I want and thank you for your assistance. Would it be possible for us to see our cabins now?"

The Purser looked down at the list he had in front of him.

"There are two cabins near each other that were not used on the outward journey," he said. "They are therefore available immediately if you would care to see them."

"Thank you, I would like to do so," Ivor replied.

They were then taken below to what Weena felt sure was the Second Class and shown their cabins.

They were indeed small but the bunks looked fairly comfortable and there was room for one trunk, but nothing else.

"These will suit my sister and me nicely," Ivor told the Purser. "Now will you please show me your secure storage room?"

They were taken to a lower deck and shown into a large dark hold where all the luggage he had brought with him could be locked up and he would be given the key.

It all took time as Ivor arranged the cases himself so that however rough the sea might become they would not be damaged in any way.

Then they went up on deck.

They had learnt from the Purser that they were not staying long in Greece.

The people who had gone ashore had already seen the notice on the way out and they were now in a hurry to go back on board ship rather than spend their time looking at Temples and the other famous sights of Athens.

Watching them now walk up the gangway, Weena thought that they looked rather dull and what her mother would have called 'middle class English'.

There were also a good few men who she was quite certain were salesmen. They sat down at once at one of the bridge tables and started to gamble amongst themselves.

There was no one, she thought, of any particular interest. They were mostly men who were very obviously travelling on business and a few elderly couples who were on holiday.

When the last passenger had come aboard, the ship began to move slowly out of Port.

"We are not full," Weena said to her brother.

"I am thankful for that," he replied. "It means that we will receive more attention and then not have to bother ourselves with talking to people who we have never seen before and will hopefully never see again."

Weena grinned.

"It's not quite as bad as that."

"They are a very dull lot as far as I can ascertain," Ivor replied. "But then we are not on one of the smart ships that are not only very expensive but have a dramatic appearance, which is what I have planned for us when we reach London!"

"You are so sure that we will be welcome," Weena remarked, "that I am just beginning to believe it myself."

"Just leave everything to me," her brother said. "I have it all worked out in my mind. I have no intention of appearing as we are right now as Mr. and Miss Dawson in whom no one, if they have any sense, would be interested for one moment."

Weena laughed.

"Now you are being unexpectedly humble!"

"I am playing the part of a dealer who has gone to Russia to find valuable objects to sell, but, when we reach England, it will be Prince Ivor Kerlensky who is selling part of his collection so that he can buy even better things. Even Russians, rich though most people think we are, do not always have the ready cash for anything they want to buy."

He paused for a moment before he added,

"I will make it clear what I am looking for and you, of course, must help me by looking beautiful all the time."

"Perhaps no one will admire me, then I will have to go back to being just an unimportant Russian or perhaps remain as an unimpressive Englishwoman!"

"I believe we will be successful in what we have set out to do," Ivor replied. "As you know, we can only look back and see the ruins of what was once our home and you can be certain by now that they will have grabbed our land and we are powerless to take any of it back."

Weena was silent for a moment.

She was thinking that she and Ivor were moving between Heaven and Hell.

They could only hope when they reached Heaven, which to him was England, it would be as wonderful as he expected it to be.

It was no use saying they had left behind everything that had been theirs since they were born and it was no use regretting that all the people they had trusted had, if not deceived them, then forgotten them.

She too, like Ivor, believed that what lay ahead was going to be marvellous and she hoped and prayed it would be.

It was on the first night at sea that Ivor found that there were some congenial men on board who asked him if he would like to join them at bridge.

"We were four when we started," they said, "but one of our friends has decided to stay in Constantinople, so if you would care to join us we would be delighted to have you."

"I should be pleased to have a game with you," Ivor replied. "Thank you for inviting me."

They moved into a room where bridge tables were laid out by the portholes, leaving Weena alone.

"Perhaps you should retire to bed," Ivor suggested. "You know as well as I do that you have had a long day and you must be feeling tired."

He did not wait for her to reply, but went after the man who had gone ahead of him.

Weena longed to say that she hoped he would not lose any money.

At the same time she felt that he was too astute to do so. He had always been very fond of bridge which he had frequently played with his father's friends even when he was quite young.

She walked towards her cabin and then she thought that she would go up on deck and say goodbye to Greece, the Gods and Goddesses and their sublime Temples.

She longed to have seen more of it all, but at least she had seen the Parthenon and thought that she would always remember the exquisite statues it contained.

Having gone up on deck she went to the bow of the ship which was now moving smoothly through the water.

It was a warm night and the moon was rising in the sky and it was pouring its bright light over the land they were leaving.

She was thinking just how beautiful it all was when she was aware that a man was walking along the deck and was just passing by her when he stopped.

She looked at him and realised that it was the same man who had helped her down from the Parthenon.

To her surprise he recognised her and exclaimed,

"It is really you! Are you now safe and sound as I hoped you would be?"

"I am still very grateful to you," Weena said. "If I had hurt myself, as I might have done, I would have had to stay in Greece rather than be here."

"But you are here and it is so delightful to see you again," the man replied.

She had been leaning on the rail and he came and stood beside her and leant on it too.

"I was thinking of you, strange to relate," he said. "In fact when I first saw you I was not certain whether you were real or one of the Greek Goddesses."

Weena smiled.

"That is a charming compliment and I should love to be one of the Goddesses. I only wish that I could have seen more of them, but my brother is in a hurry to reach London."

"So that is where you are going," he said. "I think it appropriate that we should introduce ourselves. My name is Hart, David Hart. Please tell me yours."

There was just a moment's hesitation while Weena remembered that her chosen name was now Dawson.

Then she said,

"My name is Dawson, Weena Dawson. My brother and I are travelling to London."

"Well, I only hope you get there without any sort of accident," David Hart observed.

"Thanks to you I was rescued from having a very nasty one," Weena replied. "I just cannot believe that there will be an accident on this ship unless, of course, we fall into the sea!"

David Hart laughed.

"I expect, like most people, you wanted to explore Greece, which I have just been doing. I can assure you it is still the most beautiful country in the whole world."

"You speak as though you have seen a great deal of the world," Weena commented.

"I have as it happens," he answered. "I have been journeying round seeing places that I have only read about and which I have found fascinating."

"You are very very lucky!" Weena exclaimed. "It is what I have always wanted to do myself, but have never been able to leave home until now."

"So this will be your first visit to England?"

Weena nodded.

"Do you think it will be as beautiful a country as Greece?" she asked.

As she spoke, she looked out at the hills they were passing, which she felt looked magical in the moonlight.

They were, in fact, filled with the wonders they had known in the past that were still vibrating over the world when people read about them and learnt how much Greece had brought to the civilised world.

As if he guessed what she was thinking, David Hart said,

"I love Greece. When I was quite a small boy and was told all the stories of its Gods and Goddesses by my mother, I was thrilled by them."

He paused before he went on,

"This is the third time I have visited Greece. It still has a great deal to teach me."

"How lucky you have been. I have always wanted to go to Greece and I have read so many books about it. Now I have spent a short time in the Parthenon from where you rescued me and, of course, it has made me want to see more and more."

"Which I am sure one day you will," David replied. "I think that, as I met you in Greece, to me you will always be a part of the beauty which was Greece and which is still there for us to see and admire today."

Weena smiled.

"Thank you so much, kind sir, for the compliment. And thank you once again for saving me from breaking my leg or being hurt in some other painful way."

"Perhaps it was indeed Fate like everything else in our life," David remarked. "I have often found that the most surprising things happen unexpectedly. Just as one is entranced by a treasure such as Greece, one finds another place a disappointment and not the least what you expected it to be."

"It must be very sad when you feel that you have wasted your time and your money?"

"Exactly!" David exclaimed. "I expect when you get older you find, as I have, that one is always afraid that one will not see and do everything one wants to do before one dies."

Weena laughed.

"It's asking too much to see the whole world. But at least you have been lucky to see some of it. Who could ask more than to go three times to Greece?"

"You are quite right. I am just being greedy. But I have always wanted more than I have. That is why I am exploring the world whenever I can find the opportunity."

Weena thought that he would probably have to save up for such journeys and reflected,

"I think like most people you have to be grateful for small mercies. I will be grateful when I have seen a tiny bit of Greece and hope, like you, that one day I will be able to return."

"Of course you will. Not only will you see Greece but very many other places that are often more entrancing than one expects, although on the other hand some are even more disappointing."

"Tell me about the places that are as beautiful as Greece," Weena implored him. "I have seen so little of the world and have had to be content to read about it from the books which had made me long to visit Greece."

She paused and looked a little sad as she added,

"Now I am leaving it. I did so hope that I would have a chance of seeing the Island of Delos where Apollo landed and claimed that small part of Greece for himself."

She was speaking softly because she thought at that moment, although she was not really certain, they must be passing the island where the ancient race who were called 'the Shining Ones' lived.

Not far away from them was Olympus itself where the Gods and Goddesses had met and enchanted the outside world, which had then worshipped them.

"You will see it all one day," David said quietly. "But what is important is that it is already yours because it has touched your heart and that is a magic that you will never forget."

"You are right, of course you are right. It is the things that touch one's heart that are of real significance not those you miss."

"Exactly! But so few people realise that especially when they are as young as you."

They were then both silent, as they leant over the rail gazing out towards the land they were passing.

Then Weena was aware that he was looking at her rather than at the land in front of them.

There was something in the vibrations coming from him that made her feel shy.

"My brother is playing bridge," she volunteered, "and he told me I should go to bed. I suppose that is where I should be."

"I will not beg you to stay talking to me," David replied. "As you have obviously had a long day, you must be tired. But there is always tomorrow and I hope we will be able to talk together here at any rate and, if I tell you some of the secrets of Greece, you must then tell me what you have read about all the different countries we will be passing before we reach England."

Weena thought this was something exciting which she had never expected.

"I would love that," she said. "I am so glad that we have met. I can only thank you once again for saving me."

"I have always been lucky," he answered. "Perhaps today I was even luckier than usual in that I found you."

Again there was a note in his voice which made Weena feel bashful.

She smiled at him and said,

"Goodnight."

Then without waiting for his reply she was hurrying along the deck.

When she reached the entrance to go below, she did not look back.

She only thought as she reached her own cabin that, if Ivor had enjoyed his bridge game, then she had certainly enjoyed meeting a man who understood just how much the enchanting stories of the Gods and Goddesses had always meant to her.

'This is a piece of luck I did not expect,' Weena told herself as she started to undress.

CHAPTER FOUR

The next day when Weena wanted to either read one of the books from the ship's library or hopefully talk to David, Ivor insisted that she go and watch him play deck tennis.

"I am really rather good at it," he boasted, "and I have been challenged by a man who fancies himself. So I thought you would enjoy watching me beat him."

She laughed.

"Mind you do," she urged him, "otherwise I would suppose that I will have to shed tears for you!"

She thought it would be unkind if she did not watch Ivor and she only hoped that David did not wait for her for a long time in the helm where they had met before.

Needless to say Ivor won, but not as easily as he had hoped.

His opponent was rather good as he had had more practice than Ivor, but he still managed to beat him with a tremendous effort and Weena clapped.

They talked a long time over luncheon because Ivor wanted to tell her more about what they would do when they reached England.

"The first thing," he said, "is we have to try to find a house in a smart part of London so that people will be impressed by us and not think that we are poor refugees who need to beg money from them."

"I hope we don't have to do that," Weena replied. "It is something that would have shocked Mama and Papa who would have been simply furious at the very idea."

"I agree with you," Ivor said. "But 'beggars can't be choosers' or too particular in what they can do. So we must remember that if we don't get married quickly, we are quite likely to starve – "

"Don't think about it, Ivor, it's unlucky."

"I know that, but we have to face facts and what we have managed to bring with us might keep us going for a year, but certainly no longer."

*

Later that evening when Ivor went to play bridge, Weena walked up to the deck hoping that David would be there.

However, there was no sign of him.

She thought that it would be a mistake to seem too eager and she moved away from the helm to further along the deck.

She had not gone far when one of the men who had spoken to Ivor before dinner joined her.

"I am the odd man out tonight," he began, "so I thought I would come and find you."

He was the one Weena had taken a dislike to and she knew that her mother would have thought him common.

He was however tall, fairly good-looking and with square shoulders and dark hair.

Equally there was something about him which told her that he was not a particularly attractive person and she really had no desire to be with him.

"As it so happens," she replied to him, "I was just going to bed. I feel rather tired. Perhaps it's the fresh air and I know that I will fall asleep at once."

His name was Cyril Bates and he now looked round as if to ascertain that there was no one near them.

He then said almost in a whisper,

"If you really intend to go to bed and not talk to me as I would very much like you to do, you must at least kiss me goodnight."

Weena felt shocked by his forward behaviour and therefore said quickly,

"Goodnight. I really must go to my cabin."

Cyril Bates put out his arm and pulled her close to him.

"You'll go when I let you go," he insisted. "You're very pretty, in fact the prettiest girl in the whole ship. I want you to stay here with me!"

Weena put her hands against him and tried to push him away, but he was very much taller than she was and obviously much stronger.

As he bent his head towards her, she cried out,

"Let me go!"

She began to struggle against him.

She knew only too well that she was really helpless against his greater strength.

As his lips sought hers, she moved her head sharply from side to side and gave a little scream. Even as she did so, feeling that she was helpless in Cyril's arms, a voice called out angrily,

"What is going on here?"

Weena knew at once that it was David.

And then with a tremendous effort she managed to extract herself from Cyril's arms and threw herself against David.

"Don't you dare interfere with me," Cyril said in an offensive tone. "I was here first and it's no business of yours who I am and what I'm doing!"

As he spoke, he drew back his arm as if to strike David who moved quickly.

To Weena's astonishment he hit Cyril so hard that he lost his balance and fell over backwards onto the deck.

"Damn you!" he shouted up from the floor. "I'll not have you treating me like this."

David did not answer.

He merely took Weena by the arm and walked her quickly down the deck towards the helm.

She was feeling too shaken to do or say anything.

Because he had one arm round her waist and was pulling her along with him, she walked as quickly as he wanted her to do.

They reached the helm and he then sat her down on the same seat they had sat on before, which was under the Captain's bridge.

"How on earth did you get mixed up with a fellow like that?" he asked almost angrily, as he sat down beside Weena.

"He was playing bridge with my brother," she said, "and so I spoke to him earlier. I had no idea that he would behave like that."

"He is a cad and certainly no gentleman," David said. "I suppose we must expect there to be all types of people on this sort of vessel."

He spoke scornfully and she thought that perhaps he normally travelled in large expensive ships and for this voyage he may not have wanted to waste his money.

It was, however, something she did not want to talk about.

She therefore said to David,

"Thank you! But I am afraid the man you knocked down will be very angry."

"Let him be, he was behaving abominably."

"He frightened me," Weena murmured.

"It's not at all surprising. In future you must be very careful and not be alone."

Weena managed to smile.

"That means I will have to stay in my cabin," she replied. "The moonlight is so beautiful on the sea that I had to come up on deck."

"Then you must have someone to escort you and look after you," David suggested. "That can be me until I disembark at Gibraltar."

"Is that where you are leaving the ship?" Weena asked him, trying not to sound disappointed.

"I intend to as I want to see the monkeys again and I thought of spending a short time in Portugal."

Weena smiled.

"You are so lucky and I have read about Gibraltar and, of course, Portugal, Spain and all the countries in that part of Europe. But I have never had the chance of visiting them."

"You are very young and there is plenty of time for you to visit the whole world if you wish to. It is wanting to that matters. So many people are content to sit at home and then never see and appreciate the beauty and delight of foreign lands."

"You are so fortunate to be able to travel," Weena replied. "I have had to be content with just reading books about them. There is so much I want to see that this trip in itself, simply because we are here in the Mediterranean, is an excitement that I have never experienced before."

She thought as she spoke that she was on dangerous ground.

It would be a great mistake to let anyone know exactly where they had come from or why they were going to England.

So she changed the subject by saying quickly,

"Tell me, which the most exciting country you have visited and why?"

David smiled.

"That is certainly a difficult question to answer," he replied. "I have travelled a great deal and enjoyed every minute of it. My family keeps saying that I should settle down and get married."

"But you want to see all the world before you do so," Weena remarked.

"How do you know that?" he asked.

"Because there is a note in your voice when you talk about travelling," she answered, "which tells me how much it means to you."

"Well, I have been very lucky," David admitted. "I have seen most of the East and I would love to show you some of the beauties of India and those of Siam."

"I have read about them both," Weena replied. "I also know how beautiful everyone found them."

"I think most girls of your age are worrying about how many proposals of marriage they have had and which of the men they have danced with is more attractive than the others."

Weena laughed.

But she did not tell him that she had never had a proposal of marriage nor had she been to many dances.

There had naturally been dances at Christmas time in the Caucasus, but their neighbours lived some way away from them.

And after their father became ill their mother had no wish to stay away even though most hostesses expected her to stay with them if the party did not end until late.

There was silence for a moment.

Then David said,

"I suppose if I was really gallant, as I should be, having saved you from a villain, I would stay aboard until you reach England to make sure you are safe from other dangers as well as being a stranger in a strange land."

"It is very kind of you to think of it, David," Weena replied. "But, of course, I could not be so cruel as to take you away from your exploration of enchanting lands which I have not been able to see."

She was speaking lightly as she was quite sure that he was only teasing her and he really had no intention of staying aboard the ship to protect her.

After all she had only just met him and had been fortunate that he had saved her in Athens and now again at sea.

As if he knew what she was thinking, David said,

"I suppose being so beautiful that you will get into trouble wherever you go."

As no one outside her family had ever called her beautiful before, Weena stared at him for a moment.

Then she told herself that she must not take him too seriously.

"I promise you," she said, "I will try to keep out of trouble especially the sort you have just rescued me from."

"And I have done so now for a second time," David remarked, "what would you do if I am not here?"

"I suppose I should pray that an angel would drop down from Heaven or perhaps a 'merman' will come out of the sea to protect me," Weena replied.

David chuckled as she meant him to do.

She thought to herself again that it would be a great mistake to be too serious and he was really only teasing her in saying that he had better stay and protect her.

Quickly, because she was afraid that he might think she was clinging on to him or being tiresome in some way, she said,

"What you must do if you have not done so already, is to write down your travel experiences as they happen. Eventually you will put it all into a book which everyone who has never had your good luck will want to read."

"Actually I have thought about that already," David replied unexpectedly. "But I decided it would be a waste of time now when I might be exploring. I will therefore keep my adventures in my mind until I am too old or too tied down to continue them."

"What do you mean by 'tied down'?" Weena asked. "Is there something in England which will one day keep you from going abroad?"

For a moment there was silence.

Weena felt that by mistake she had asked a question that he had no wish to answer or which embarrassed him.

'He might be married and perhaps have a number of children,' she thought to herself.

Because she had no wish for him to think that she was prying on him, she rose to her feet.

"I really think I must retire to bed," she said. "I am very tired. I would be grateful if you would walk with me as far as the companionway in case I encounter that man you knocked down."

"Of course I will accompany you if that is what you want," David replied. "But I rather hoped we could go on talking here. I am travelling alone, as I usually do, but I seldom find someone as congenial as you are to discuss the journey with or who is as interested as you are in the places I have already visited."

"I want you to tell me about all of them," Weena said. "But I think I should go to bed now."

David rose to his feet.

As they walked side by side along the deck, Weena thought that she was being very silly in leaving him when he obviously did not want her to do so.

She was not certain how soon they would arrive in Gibraltar, but she had a feeling that it would be perhaps late tomorrow or the next day.

Then she would never see him again.

As they reached the door that led into the ship, she longed to say that she had changed her mind and wanted to stay with him.

Then she felt that it would seem uncomfortable if she did so.

So she merely said,

"Goodnight, David, and thank you very very much for being so kind to me."

Before he could answer her, she then ran down the companionway that led to her cabin.

*

The next day Ivor had no wish to play deck tennis so he took Weena on an exploration of the ship.

He showed her the top deck and the lower deck and they went down to the engine room.

She was fascinated by it all.

But she could not help wishing that she was with David and talking to him about the beautiful sights to be found in foreign lands.

After luncheon, which was drawn out because two of the men Ivor had played bridge with came and talked to them, Weena went on deck hoping to find David.

But he was nowhere to be seen.

After looking round for a while, because she was afraid of running into the dreadful Cyril Bates again, she went to her cabin.

She lay down on the bunk bed and read the book she had taken from the library.

It was quite interesting, but not so well written as the books that had been in her father's library.

Later that night there was to be a performance after dinner given by a travelling group of musicians and Ivor agreed to go and, of course, his sister accompanied him.

It was a very good performance as the musicians were well known in a great many Capitals of Europe.

At the same time she could not help but wish that she was talking to David, but there was no sign of him at the concert.

*

The next day they arrived at Gibraltar.

Weena thought with a strange feeling that she had not felt before that she was losing something very precious.

It was here that David was to leave the ship.

Whatever happened she was determined to say her goodbyes to him.

She went up on deck to watch the other people who were disembarking, but David was not amongst them.

She learnt from the Purser that they would not be staying very long in Gibraltar, but would be leaving in the afternoon.

She was afraid that David would get off at luncheon time or perhaps earlier and she would miss him altogether.

'I wonder where he could possibly be?' she asked herself, but could find no answer to her question.

Then just as the ship seemed to be on the verge of leaving and the gangways were being pulled up, she saw with a thrill in her heart that David was coming aboard.

It was with difficulty that she did not run towards him and throw her arms round him and she told herself that she must behave properly.

It was disgraceful for a young woman to run after a man and she was expected, as her mother had always told her, to behave like a lady.

Therefore she moved a little further along the deck.

She felt her heart leap when he stepped aboard, but he did not go below as she thought he would do.

Instead of which he came towards her.

Despite her effort not to show what she was feeling, as he reached her, Weena heard herself saying,

"I thought you had left without saying goodbye."

"I only went ashore to cancel the arrangement I had already made," he replied, "and to buy you a small present. I thought that you deserved one as, although the ship was staying here for a short time, you were not able to explore Gibraltar yourself."

David handed her a parcel as he spoke.

"A present!" Weena exclaimed, "how very kind of you. Of course I would have loved to have seen Gibraltar properly, but Ivor did not want to go ashore and I was too nervous to go alone."

"I would have taken you," David said, "but I had a great number of matters to see to, so I left the ship very early."

He paused before he added,

"Now open your present and see if it pleases you."

Weena undid the wrapping which was not very strong.

She found that he had given her one of the beautiful Chinese shawls she had heard were obtainable in Gibraltar.

It was embroidered with pink and blue flowers and she thought that it was the loveliest shawl she had ever seen.

"Is it really for me?" she asked, "how very kind of you, David. Thank you, thank you a thousand times!"

"I thought you would like it. It will remind you of Gibraltar and the Mediterranean and, of course, how we met each other in Greece."

"It's absolutely lovely!" she cried, touching the silk roses with her fingers. "How could you be so generous?"

"You should always have a souvenir of every place you visit," David told her. "Maybe one day you will come back and see the monkeys and, of course, the shops which are filled with attractive objects from China."

"I don't know how to thank you," Weena sighed.

"I think you will need it tonight and every night because, as we sail nearer to England, then it will become colder. So it is a practical as well as a pretty present."

"Of course it is and easily the prettiest one I have ever had. I have read about the beautiful embroidery that comes from China, which no one except the Chinese can work so well or so expertly."

"That is right," David agreed. "Now I will tell you a little more about China. It is one of the countries that I visited two years ago."

They sat down in their usual place in the helm.

As the ship began to move slowly out of the Port of Gibraltar, Weena held the beautiful shawl on her lap and listened intently to everything that David had to tell her.

They met there again the next day and then the sea became very rough and the ship was tossed from wave to wave like a feather duster.

It was just impossible for Weena to leave her cabin. She wanted to do so, but Ivor was firm about it.

"You don't want to break your leg just as we are arriving in London," he admonished her. "There is nothing more dangerous than walking about when the sea is really rough. You are to stay here and I will fetch any books you want."

He paused for a moment before he added,

"I want you to look really beautiful when we arrive at London and not be hobbling about on one leg!"

Because she had to obey him, Weena tried to do so with a smile.

She felt she was missing something very precious in not being able to talk more with David and not to be able to show him how becoming his Chinese shawl was on her.

The ship called briefly at Lisbon, but there was no time to go ashore and explore the City.

Later it seemed as if the time they spent pitching and tossing in the storm was endless.

She reckoned that there would only be two days after the sea became calmer for her to leave her cabin and find David.

She wondered if she should write him a short note.

Then she decided that the least she could do was to send him a letter of thanks for the wonderful present he had given her.

Because she thought it was correct to only write a very conventional letter to someone she hardly knew, she merely thanked him for the marvellous present.

She said how sorry she was that she could not wear it at the moment because the sea was too rough for her to leave her cabin.

It was only when she had finished the letter and signed her name did she put as a PS,

"I am wrapping your present round my shoulders and telling myself a Fairy story about it!"

She thought that he would understand and not think that she was too pushy or trying to obtain another present from him.

Then the ship was pitching and tossing violently, so that it was impossible for her to even get out of her bed.

When finally the sea did calm and they reached the English Channel, she climbed out of bed and hurried up on deck.

It was a day with little sunshine and everything was damp because it had rained during the night.

And she hoped, however, that she would see David waiting for her somewhere near the helm.

But no one was there.

When she went back into the ship he was not, as she hoped, in the library or in the Saloon.

Nor was there any sign, and she was very glad, of the unpleasant man who had tried to kiss her.

She then learnt that Ivor had made new friends at the bridge table.

Finally, because she wanted to see David so much and also because there was still no sign of him and she was afraid that he might be ill, she went to call on the Purser.

"Is a gentleman by the name of David Hart still on the ship?" she enquired.

The Purser looked down at the papers he had beside him.

"Hart? Hart?" he asked himself beneath his breath. "Yes, here we are, that gentleman left the ship at Lisbon. I ought to have remembered as he was the only passenger who left us at that Port."

Weena gave a deep sigh.

He had gone and she had not said goodbye to him.

At least he had her letter saying how grateful she was, but she wanted to see him in the flesh.

And to talk to him as they had before about the wonderful places he had visited which she was sure now she would never see.

"We will be in Port the day after tomorrow," her brother said that evening, "and then we will really start our adventure."

"Yes, of course," Weena replied unenthusiastically.

She wondered why she did not feel as thrilled about it all as she had before.

The weather was warmer and the sun was shining brightly as they steamed up the Channel and into the North Sea before they found the opening into the Thames.

Weena realised that her brother was becoming more excited with every hour that passed.

"We have had a major stroke of luck," he told her the night before they arrived.

"What is that, Ivor?" she asked.

"I found that one of the men on the ship is an agent for houses to be sold or rented in London."

"Is that what we are going to do?" Weena enquired.

"Yes, of course. I have told you before that I intend for us to descend on London as rich and important people and naturally we have no wish to go round begging to be put up."

He spoke quite crossly and Weena said,

"I am sorry but you did not tell me exactly where we will be staying in London and I did not want to worry you by asking silly questions."

"It's not a silly question but a sensible one," her brother answered. "I think this man has the very thing we want."

"What is that?" she asked.

"He told me that he has on his list of houses to be rented or sold, one in Park Lane which is, of course, one of the most prestigious streets in London."

Weena was listening to him, but she did not like to ask questions.

Then her brother went on,

"It overlooks Hyde Park and it is very unusual for any of the houses to be empty. The one he has available is in bad disrepair but, because it needs a great deal of money spent on it, the rent is cheap. But it still makes anyone who is living in it of Social significance."

"Can we afford the rent for it?" Weena asked.

"We can afford it and it will make us noticed which is the right way to start. Besides which, as you well know, I have the list of Prince Feodor's friends to write to, to tell them how eager we are to meet them."

"They might easily think us rather pushy," Weena commented.

"Not the way I will word it," her brother replied. "With our titles and an excellent address to introduce us, we will soon be riding high in English Society."

He spoke with such enthusiasm in his voice and in such a positive manner that Weena could only hope that he was not exaggerating the situation.

And that he was in fact doing the right thing rather than playing a game of pretence or what her mother would have thought to be a series of lies.

Yet what was the alternative?

They had no home to go back to.

Maybe already many of their friends were suffering in the same way as they had suffered.

They had managed to go away relatively unscathed, but other people might have had their houses burnt down and save nothing from the destruction and so had nowhere to go.

"I think it is very clever of you," she said aloud to her brother, "to have found a house so quickly. That will save us money as I am sure the hotels are very expensive."

"As I have already told you we have enough money and enough items to sell to keep us for at least a year in great comfort," he replied sharply. "If by that time we have not found all that we are seeking, then we will be very stupid indeed."

Weena knew he was thinking that they must both marry money.

She felt herself shudder at the idea.

Then she thought about how David had saved her from the man who had tried to kiss her and how if he had not been there the man would have done so.

She knew she would have been not only shocked and upset but disgusted because there was something very unpleasant about him.

It now struck her for the first time that perhaps Ivor would insist on her marrying someone who was rich but for whom she had no feeling and someone with whom she had nothing in common.

She might even be repulsed by him.

Because she was very innocent and her knowledge of the world relied entirely on the books she had read, Weena knew little or nothing about men.

She had no idea what she would feel if a man made love to her.

She only knew that the man who had tried to kiss her had seemed repulsive.

She would always be eternally grateful to David because he had saved her from the horror of it.

But David had gone and now she had to face the Social world which she knew nothing about.

According to her brother's instructions she had to marry someone who might be as unpleasant and repulsive as the man who had tried to kiss her on the ship.

Going to London had seemed very exciting until now and the thrill of it had been very much the same as being told that she was going to India, China or Paris.

Now she was suddenly afraid of what she would find in London and what the future would hold for her if she obeyed her brother.

'How can I marry any man just because he is rich?' she asked herself, but there was no answer.

There was no one she could discuss what she knew was one of the largest and most intimidating projects she had ever encountered.

The ship came to a halt by the Tower of London.

There were quite a number of people to go ashore and most of them were ready to leave the ship the moment the anchors went down.

Ivor, however, insisted that there was no hurry as he wanted his precious possessions taken ashore with every possible care and to make certain that nothing was broken.

They therefore waited until almost every passenger had left before Ivor's treasures were taken out of the hold where they had been housed.

They were stacked onto a carriage and they took up so much room that a second carriage had to be ordered for him and Weena.

The agent was to travel with them and they set off first with their possessions following behind.

"You will find everything you need in the house except servants," the agent was saying. "But you must not be too depressed at the state it's in, having been empty for over two years."

"I am surprised no one has taken it," Ivor answered. "But, of course, as I have already told you, I want only the best."

"Houses in Park Lane are hard to come by," the agent informed him. "And the same applies to Grosvenor Square and other fashionable parts of London."

He paused and smiled as he added,

"Of course you could go to Islington or somewhere like that, but they are not so smart and that, I understand, is what you want."

"Now we have left the ship," Ivor said, "I will let you into our little secret. My sister and I are deliberately travelling incognito so that people will not take too much notice of us."

"Incognito!" the agent then exclaimed. "And why should you do that, sir?"

"Because we are actually Russian Royalty and we were told before we left that it was a great mistake for us to give our Royal names on the ship so that we were made not only a great fuss of but were charged at least double."

The agent laughed.

"That be true. They put the prices up for anyone who they think can afford it and I wondered myself when you asked me for a smart house how you would pay for it."

"You need not worry about that," Ivor told him in a lofty tone. "Actually, now that we are clear of the ship, I will introduce myself as Prince Ivor and my sister's name is Princess Alweena Kerlensky."

The agent stared at them for a moment.

Then he said,

"Well, I can understand, Your Highness, why you did it and it's very clever of you too, if I might say so."

"Thank you," Ivor said. "I feel I am very fortunate in being able to obtain this house from you, if it pleases my sister and, of course, we will pay what you asked before you knew who I was."

The agent laughed.

"You have been very astute indeed, Your Highness. I would certainly have doubled the rent if I had known who you were. Not that we expects the Russians as a rule to be as rich as them Americans be!"

"Are the Americans very rich?" Ivor enquired as if it was of no consequence.

"They're rich enough," the agent replied. "Most of them throw it all about in the wrong way. It seems such a waste in my opinion."

"I am sure it would be in mine too," Ivor answered. "Let me assure you that things are not very stable now in Russia, which is why my sister and I have come away. We have no wish to waste what money we have. So please do not tempt us into spending unnecessarily."

"You can trust me, Your Highness. I can assure you my Company is one of the best in London. In fact, to be honest, I were expecting you to say you wanted something small and cheap."

Ivor chuckled.

"As it is," he said, "it is something large and also cheap!"

"That is exactly what I am offering you," the agent replied. "When you see it, it may look a bit dusty, but that can soon be cleaned up. If you ask me it's a snip. If you don't agree with me, I'll be really disappointed."

He spoke so earnestly that Weena laughed.

But she knew that her brother was delighted with the fact that they were to have a house in the smartest and most fashionable part of London.

It was, in his opinion, exactly the right way to start them off on their voyage of discovery.

CHAPTER FIVE

After spending some time knocking on the door of the house, it was opened by an elderly man with white hair.

When he saw who accompanied them, he said to the agent.

"Oh, there you be Mr. Jones. I'm sorry I kept you waitin', but we were in the kitchen havin' trouble with the stove and I didn't hear the door at first."

"It's all right, Brownlow," the agent replied. "I've brought two potential customers who I hope will be taking over the house."

It certainly was dusty, as the agent had told them, and the windows needed cleaning.

As they went round, Weena could see that it was just the sort of background her brother needed if he was to impress English Society.

The rooms were large and had obviously been well furnished before they became unused and therefore had a run-down appearance.

But Weena was certain that the colour would come back on the covers and the curtains once the accumulated dust was shaken off them.

On the ground floor there was a very nice drawing room, a study that she was certain her brother would want to use and a music room with an ancient grand piano.

To her delight there was a library and books filled the shelves right up to the ceiling.

She thought with joy that even if she was not going to be a success in Society, she would at least have plenty to read.

They only had a quick glance at the rooms before the agent hurried them upstairs to see what he insisted were the very best rooms.

The drawing room was indeed double the size of any other room they had seen.

When it was first in use, it must have been most impressive, but now it looked somewhat dingy.

But Weena thought that it would not be too difficult to bring it back to perfection.

The drawing room was located on the first floor and so were the best bedrooms.

The Master bedroom, which she knew her brother would want to occupy, had an enormous bed with a canopy and curtains of red velvet.

It was essentially a man's room and opening out of it was a boudoir which the agent explained was used by the Master and Mistress of the house.

It had a very fine French secretaire by the window and leading off the boudoir there was a pretty bedroom with a four-poster bed carved in gilt with curtains in yellow chintz.

There was a dressing table with a muslin petticoat round it and a gold mirror ornamented with golden cupids.

Weena did not have to tell Ivor how delighted she was with the house and she knew from the expression on his face that it was exactly what he desired.

But he was very determined to rent it as cheaply as he possibly could.

"I will certainly rent the house," he said, "but you will have to let me have it somewhat cheaper because there is so much work to be done before it is useable."

He saw that the agent was about to refuse and went on,

"I intend to entertain the most important people in Society here, who I already have an introduction to from my friends and, of course, from the Czar of Russia. When I vacate it, you will obviously get double or treble what you are asking now because I will have spent so much time and money on it."

He saw that the agent was taking in what he was saying.

After a considerable pause, he replied,

"I will let Your Highness have it very cheaply for the first six months, after that it would be only fair for us to double the price we are asking."

Watching her brother, Weena was quite certain that he would achieve his ambition in the first six months.

After that the money would be of no interest.

She could not help but think that he was gambling in a somewhat reckless manner, but at the same time they had nowhere else to go.

Again a feeling of misery swept over her because she had lost not only her father and her lovely home but also the beauty of their surroundings.

Nowhere in the world, she had always been told, were the trees as magnificent or as beautiful as they were in the Caucasus and it was doubtful if she would ever see them again.

Then she told herself that it was no use looking back, she had to look forward.

Forward meant helping Ivor in his plans for them both to marry money so that they would be sure to be safe and comfortable for the rest of their lives.

Ivor was, in fact, already sitting at the secretaire near the window and signing the contract that the agent had taken from his pocket.

"Now perhaps, Your Highness," he suggested, "you would wish to stay for a night or two in a hotel while this house is readied for you."

"That would surely be a needless extravagance," he replied somewhat harshly. "We will stay here and work, I can now assure you, far harder than anyone else, to make this place spick and span before I ask my friends to visit me."

He finished signing the cheque which he had taken from his briefcase.

He handed it to the agent saying,

"All I want you to tell me please is where I engage servants and, of course, a cleaner to clear up this mess."

"You won't have to look far, Your Highness," the agent replied. "Brownlow will be able to tell you that the best Domestic Agency in London is just round the corner in Oxford Street. I'm sure they'll be only too pleased to send you anyone you require."

"Thank you," Ivor said, "it's all I need to know. I am very grateful to you for your help and it was extremely fortunate for me that we were on the same ship together."

"I am the one who is the most fortunate!" the agent exclaimed. "We've been trying to get rid of this house for over a year. There's always been the same excuse from those we take round it. It's too big and too dilapidated."

"Well, I am the exception," Ivor laughed. "I hope you will call and see us when we have transformed it into what we want it to be."

The agent thanked him again.

Having shaken hands both with him and Weena, he hurried downstairs and left the house.

Ivor walked into the drawing room and then stood looking at it as if he was calculating exactly what had to be done to make it presentable.

Because she felt she must encourage him, Weena slipped her arm through his.

"It's not as bad as it looks," she said. "There is inches of dust on everything which makes it all look drab. But the carpets are in a reasonably good condition and so is the furniture and the covers on the sofa and the chairs."

Ivor now seemed to be making up his mind about something.

Then he said,

"Come downstairs. I want to talk to that man who let us in. If he has been a butler here, he is exactly what we want."

Weena had hardly noticed the man except that she had seen that his hair was white and he was getting on in years.

He had been poorly dressed with an apron over his trousers and she wondered why Ivor seemed so interested in him.

However, she followed her brother downstairs.

When they reached the hall, Brownlow was closing the door having let the agent out.

He was about to speak when Ivor said,

"I want you to come with me into the study as I have a number of instructions to give you."

"You mean me wife and I can stay on – ?" the man asked impulsively.

Then as an afterthought, as if he remembered what the agent must have told him, he added,

" – Your Highness."

"I understand from the man who just left, that you used to be the butler here," Ivor began.

"Indeed I were," Brownlow replied. "And me wife was the senior cook with three scullions under her. The gentleman who employed us, Lord Malmesbury, died and we've been here as caretakers ever since always hopin' that someone like yourself would come along and open up the house again."

"That is exactly what I am going to do," Ivor told him. "So let me sit down while I talk to you."

He walked ahead with Weena beside him into the study.

He opened the window to let in some fresh air and sunshine and then he sat down at the writing desk.

As he did so, he passed his hand over the blotter and a cloud of dust rose from it.

Because it seemed so funny, Weena gave out a little laugh.

But her brother merely indicated a chair in front of the fire and she sat down.

Brownlow had followed them into the room and now he closed the door.

"What I want you to do," Ivor said, "is to go to the Domestic Agency, which I understand is near here and ask them to provide exactly what staff is necessary to put this house in running order as quickly as possible."

Brownlow stared at him.

"You really mean me – to do it, Your Highness!" he spluttered.

"Of course," Ivor replied. "I am a Russian from the Caucasus and I had a big house in the country. But I have not dealt with English servants who I am sure are different in every way from the Russians."

"I'm afraid they be very different, Your Highness."

"That is why I need to leave it all in your hands to provide us with two or three footmen, however many staff your wife requires in the kitchen and some housemaids to clean up the house and make the rooms ready for me to entertain and have people to stay if necessary."

Watching Brownlow as her brother was speaking to him, Weena thought that with every word he seemed to grow younger and to change from an old man, who no one wanted, to the efficient and respected butler he had been in the past.

When he spoke, his voice seemed clearer than it had been when he had been talking to them upstairs.

"I knows exactly what you want, Your Highness, and I'll go immediately and find out who's available."

"The sooner the better," Ivor replied. "My sister and I will stay here and perhaps, when you return from the Agency, your wife and you will be kind enough to make up the beds in the Master's and Mistress's rooms comfortable enough for tonight."

"You leave it all to me, Your Highness," Brownlow said. "I'll do everything I can and I know the Missus will start right away cleanin' up the room for Her Highness."

"Thank you. That is all I want and I am content to leave it in your experienced hands."

It seemed to Weena as if Brownlow had suddenly grown a foot taller.

As he walked to the door, he turned and asked,

"Will Your Highness be dinin' here tonight?"

"I think it would be asking too much of you," Ivor answered. "So if you can recommend a good hotel or a restaurant nearby, we will dine out."

"That be ever so considerate of Your Highness," he replied, "and I can assure you my wife's an excellent cook when she's got the right ingredients."

When he had finished speaking, Brownlow bowed and left the room.

As they heard him hurrying off down the passage, Weena laughed and said,

"You have made one person very happy, Ivor. He seemed to become at least twenty years younger when you had finished speaking to him."

"It was obviously a comedown for him to be only the caretaker here," Ivor replied. "But I expect like us they have nowhere else to go."

Weena walked to the window.

"Can we really afford to stay in this lovely house," she asked, "and to entertain as you have said so often that I have begun to believe it?"

"That is what we have come here for. I intend to entertain the best Nobility in England, also, as you already know, to find a wife for myself and a husband for you."

Weena gave a shudder.

She thought again, although she did not say so, that it would be terrifying and perhaps repulsive to marry a man she did not love simply because he had money.

But this was certainly not the right time for her to argue with her brother.

So she merely said,

"I will go and explore a little more of the house. You must tell me what time you want to leave for dinner."

"There is no hurry," Ivor told her. "If you want me to carry one of your cases upstairs, I will do so."

"Let's hope it is for the last time," Weena smiled, "and a footman will be here do it in future."

Ivor carried two of her smaller cases upstairs to the bedroom he had chosen for her.

She opened the cases and then shut them up again.

There was so much dust in the room that she knew she would be very unwise to take anything out which was not absolutely necessary.

Even then it was certain that dust would settle on it the moment she set it down on a table.

She even had to wipe the mirror on the dressing table before she could see her reflection in it.

She thought that once everything was cleaned up it would be the most beautiful bedroom she had ever slept in.

When she went downstairs, she found Ivor sitting at the writing table with a pile of letters in front of him.

"Are those all the people you are writing to?" she asked him even though she knew the answer.

"They are all the people I have learnt were friends of Prince Feodor and I intend to post them immediately so that our invitations should be pouring in by the end of the week."

"There is nothing like being optimistic, Ivor. What is more you must tell me everything you know about the Prince, otherwise they will suspect at once that he was not so much of a friend as you pretend him to be."

"I am not a fool!" Ivor snapped. "I have already looked up before we left home everything that I could find about him and his family. I also, as I have told you, met him once when I was in St. Petersburg."

"Was he very charming?" Weena enquired.

"He was certainly very impressive and that is the reputation he has in England which we will benefit from."

She thought again that he was being optimistic, but considered it a mistake to say so.

She therefore helped him put stamps on the letters which apparently he had bought from the Captain of the ship.

Then she waited at the door while he ran out to post them in the nearest post-box he could find.

When he came back, he said to her,

"Now that we have taken the first step in the right direction, we can only hope that the angels are with us!"

"I think we have been very lucky already," Weena replied.

Then she was thinking once again of how lucky she had been when David had saved her from the horrible man on the ship, and how interesting she had found him when she might have been left alone with no one to talk to while Ivor was playing bridge.

'But he did not say goodbye to me,' she reflected a little wistfully.

Then she tried to put him out of her mind because she had so much to think about.

But it was difficult.

They enjoyed an excellent dinner at a restaurant recommended by Brownlow.

*

On their return to the house they found that he had came back from the Agency to tell them that he had been extremely fortunate.

He had engaged three housemaids who would start tomorrow to clean up the house and there would be two footmen, one of whom was quite experienced.

He had also found two people to help in the kitchen and was promised that another would be arriving before the end of the week.

"My wife's now feelin' as if she's dancin' on air," Brownlow enthused. "Once we buy the food she needs, you'll have the best meals of anyone in this area."

"That is what we are looking forward to," Ivor told him. "That reminds me you must tell me what money you require to purchase the food and, of course, the cleaning materials for the house."

He paused for a moment before he added,

"I have some I can give you at once and the rest will be in the bank when I require it."

It was then that he remembered when he went into the hall that the luggage and boxes he had brought from their home still had to be unpacked and displayed.

"What we really need," he said to Weena, "are two or three men from a shop who are used to handling such valuable pictures and ornaments and will therefore display them better than any servant could do."

"I expect it will be easy for you to find out which is the best shop in this part of London," Weena replied. "Of course there must be one."

"I expect there will be a dozen if we look for them and I must go to an auctioneer to ask what they think of the pictures. Unless they value them for a very large sum of money, I will have to sell them privately."

Weena wondered what would happen if they could not sell them at all.

But her brother was speaking so optimistically that he would get what he wanted that she knew she must not appear to be in any way doubtful.

Her bed which had been made up by Brownlow and his wife was actually very comfortable.

Because there was still a distinct smell of dust in the bedroom, Weena opened all the windows and she knew by the morning that it would be very different from what it was at the moment.

She was so tired after all the excitement of the day and the worry at the back of her mind as to what the future held that she fell asleep almost as soon as her head touched the pillow.

*

When she awoke, the sun was streaming in through the open window and when she sat up in bed she could see the trees in Hyde Park.

She wondered if Ivor had slept as well as she had.

She went through the boudoir to his bedroom and found that he had already dressed and gone downstairs.

'He is certainly in a hurry to make a good start,' she thought and went back to her own room to dress.

When she finally went downstairs, it was to find that there were already two women and two men cleaning the hall and the study.

She knew that at least some of Brownlow's orders were being carried out.

She found Ivor in the dining room, which they had not seen last night.

It was a panelled room with a very fine fireplace and crystal chandeliers on either side of it.

Ivor was eating his breakfast and he looked up and exclaimed,

"Good morning, Alweena. I was wondering when you would wake up."

"Then you should have woken me," Weena replied, walking towards him. "And I had forgotten that I now had a new name!"

"Then don't you forget it again!" Ivor said sharply. "You are Princess Alweena Kerlensky and it would be a great mistake to show in any way that you were unfamiliar with your importance and Social position."

Weena laughed.

"It's like living in a dream or perhaps playing a part on the stage."

"Whichever way you find it," Ivor urged her, "you must not forget your lines. It is an imperative order that you have to obey."

"Stop frightening me, Ivor, and let me have some breakfast," Weena chided. "I see there is a bell beside you which I am sure you are expected to ring."

Ivor did as she suggested.

Brownlow, looking very different from the way he had yesterday, entered and he was now dressed exactly as an English butler should be.

He bowed as he greeted Weena,

"Good morning, Your Highness. Would you prefer eggs and bacon or fish for your breakfast? And is it tea or coffee?"

"The fish sounds delicious," Weena replied, "and I would love coffee."

Brownlow bowed again and left the room.

She said in a whisper to Ivor,

"He is marvellous and is quite obviously enjoying himself."

"He certainly is," Ivor agreed, "already servants are pouring in to clean up the house and we should be able to entertain here far sooner than I expected."

"Except we have no idea who we should entertain," Weena remarked.

"We will surely find out soon enough," he replied confidently. "In fact I will be disappointed if I don't have one or two answers to my letters today."

"You are very confident," Weena laughed. "Dare we leave the house long enough to go into the Park? I can see it through the windows and I am longing to go to Green

Park and see Rotten Row where Mama used to ride when she was a girl. She told me that all the smart young people gather there on their horses."

"Then, of course, we will have to ride there too," Ivor replied.

Weena stared at him.

"Do you really mean that or are you saying it just to be impressive?"

"Of course I mean it. I had forgotten about Rotten Row. I went there when I was in London and Mama was right. It is very smart and all the best people are mounted. I am sure that Brownlow will be able to tell us where we will be able to hire some horses before I have time to buy them at Tattersalls."

Weena stared at him in consternation.

"Oh, do be careful," she pleaded. "If you throw all our money away too soon, we will then have to leave this comfortable house and camp in Hyde Park!"

Her brother laughed.

"It will not be as bad as that. Not once people can see the treasures I have brought with me, which we have to arrange as soon as possible."

He stopped for a moment before he went on,

"Actually I see that there are one or two frames in the house which will fit the pictures I have brought with me. At the moment they are occupied by pictures which are not as beautiful or as valuable as mine."

"That will certainly save you from buying frames," Weena said. "At the same time when we leave you will have to put back the pictures that belong to the house and it would be a shame if they were damaged or lost."

"Of course it would be," her brother agreed, "but you can trust me to be careful and although you might not think it, I am counting every penny, expecting that every penny I spend will come back to me a hundredfold!"

"I only hope that's true," Weena sighed.

As she spoke, Brownlow came in with her breakfast which she found was delicious and served on silver dishes.

"Has the last tenant," she asked Ivor once they were alone, "left everything here including his silver? Surely his relations would have taken it?"

"According to Brownlow they took most of it, but they have been anxious to let the house, which they have until now been unable to do and they have left things like silver dishes and china ornaments to encourage any tenant who is interested."

"Which we certainly are," Weena laughed.

Then her smile vanished as she said,

"Oh, Ivor, I do wish we could have brought Papa's silver with us. That will all be buried now in the ruins of the house. You must remember how pretty it was because Mama had chosen it when they were first married."

"I have been telling myself ever since we left that I was a fool not to have taken away more, but it was very important that I should not show I was aware the house was going to be burnt down. I only managed to remove the things I have here at the dead of night."

"It was very brave of you to do so," Weena said, "and I am not complaining. It's just that I hate to think of the lovely treasures that meant so much to us all our lives are now lying in ashes under the smouldering remains of our glorious home."

"Don't think about it," her brother ordered. "You must look happy and cheerful and forget everything except that we two are fascinating and aristocratic Russians whom everyone wants to entertain."

"We can only hope that is what they will think," Weena said. "At the same time I am so frightened of doing the wrong thing and letting you down."

"You will only need to be your beautiful self," he replied. "And thank God that we had an English mother."

He was silent for a moment before he added,

"It would have been far more difficult for us if we did not speak perfect English and if we did not look, both of us, more English than Russian. I am convinced in my own mind that in consequence of this the English will be impressed by our title and find us extremely intriguing."

Weena giggled.

"You are certainly optimistic if nothing else. I can only promise you that, if things go wrong and you don't get exactly what you want it, will not be my fault."

"That is what I want you to say," Ivor replied.

When they had finished breakfast, they went to the study to find that the morning newspapers were arranged, as Weena thought they should be, on the stool in front of the fireplace.

"Brownlow must have ordered them all for us," she said. "Now we can look in *The Times* and *The Morning Post* and see what parties are taking place every night and hope that our names will soon be on the list."

"They will be, that I can promise!" Ivor declared.

As she picked up one of the papers, Weena had the feeling that he was convincing himself more than worrying about convincing her.

As it happened, they were making up their minds whether they would go to Rotten Row to see the horses or wait until they appeared there themselves on horseback.

"Fortunately I have a very smart riding habit that Mama had made for me before she died," Weena said. "It almost seemed too smart when I was riding at home round the fields. But now I am sure it is exactly what I want. As I know riding clothes don't go out of fashion like other clothes."

"What we require first are horses," Ivor replied. "I must find out from Brownlow where the best local stable is. There must be one in this part of London."

He was just about to ring the bell for Brownlow, when he came into the room carrying a silver salver.

"This has just been left by hand, Your Highness," he said to Ivor.

Ivor looked at the letter and picked it up quickly.

"The first reply!" he exclaimed. "I was hoping that one would arrive today."

Weena did not ask how he knew what it was before he opened it.

She merely waited patiently until he had slit open the envelope and taken out the letter.

He glanced at it before he gave a whoop of joy.

"What does it say?" Weena asked breathlessly.

"It's from Lady Carstairs, who I can assure you is one of the most famed London hostesses. She says,

'My dear Prince Ivor,

I was delighted to receive your letter this morning and to know that a friend of our dear Prince Feodor is in London.

I think of him so often and miss him more than I can say in words.

I very much hope that you and your sister are free this evening as I have a dinner party planned for young people so that they can dance afterwards.

I will look forward to meeting you and your sister at seven-thirty and please be kind enough to let the bearer of this letter bring me back your reply.

Yours sincerely,

Alice Carstairs'."

Having read it aloud, Ivor then said,

"I told you that those who had feted Prince Feodor would be pleased to meet us. I will now send a note of acceptance back with the messenger."

He opened a drawer and found that there was some headed writing paper in it besides envelopes that matched.

He then rapidly scribbled out an acceptance to Lady Carstairs while Brownlow waited.

Ivor addressed the envelope and handed it to him.

"Please tell your wife that we will be out to dinner tonight," he told him.

The butler's eyes twinkled.

"I thought that was what Your Highness would say. I can assure you that her Ladyship's parties are the best and the most envied in the whole of Mayfair."

He did not wait for an answer, but left the room closing the door behind him.

Ivor threw up his arms.

"*We have won*! We have won! Now we have been asked, as you have just heard, to dine with one of the top hostesses in the whole of Mayfair and who could ask for a better introduction to the Social world?"

"I am incredibly glad for your sake, Ivor," Weena commented.

"This is where our great adventure begins. As luck is with us, it will end with a fanfare of trumpets!"

It was Brownlow who found a good hairdresser for Weena and it was Mrs. Brownlow who pressed the dress she chose to wear.

Weena did not dare trust such a job to one of the housemaids until she could assess their capabilities.

*

In the afternoon, after they had had luncheon, they went to find a stable where they could hire horses to ride in Rotten Row tomorrow morning.

"Perhaps we will be too tired," Weena suggested.

"Then I will ride alone," Ivor asserted. "But I will make it clear to everyone I talk to that I am waiting to visit Tattersalls to buy horses to fill our own stable which is in the Mews behind us."

Weena drew in her breath.

She had the feeling that her brother was moving too quickly.

Buying horses was undoubtedly spending money he could ill afford, but she knew it was no use her continually nagging at him.

She only hoped that they would soon be able to sell their pictures and the other objects they had brought with them for the high prices he was eagerly anticipating.

She also hoped that their expenditure would not be as frightening as it appeared to be at the moment.

She next found herself wondering what happened to foreigners who came to England and then found that they were bankrupt and could not pay their bills.

Although she dared not ask Ivor the answer to this question, it consistently haunted her during the day.

He not only ordered horses for them both to ride but a carriage drawn by a pair which was to be always at their disposal and not hired to anyone else.

'Supposing,' she said to herself, as the housemaids brought her bath into her bedroom, 'we suddenly find that we have run out of money. The only course then would be for us to run away.'

She had the feeling, however, that they might send the Police after them and she remembered reading many books in which criminals were always caught and punished for their crimes.

When the hairdresser came to arrange her hair in the very latest fashion, she told herself that she was being stupid.

What she had to do was to relax and enjoy herself.

As her brother had told her, she must find herself a husband as soon as possible so that their debts would no longer be a threat.

She could not imagine anything more humiliating than having to ask the man she married to pay her bills almost before she bore his name.

At the same time she tried not to go into details of what Ivor was doing, but to believe that he knew it was the only possible way to live in the future as he wanted to live.

When finally her hair was arranged and she was dressed in a very pretty gown that her mother had bought for her, she thought that at least Ivor would not be ashamed of her.

"You look lovely, really lovely, Your Highness," the hairdresser cooed. "I can only say that at your first ball in London you will undoubtedly be the belle of it!"

"I do hope so," Weena replied, "and thank you very much for doing my hair so beautifully. I would love you to come again."

"I expect you'll be wanting me every day and every night," the hairdresser answered. "I will be very surprised if I'm not right in what I foretell for your future."

"I will be very sad if I disappoint you, so thank you again for making me look so good."

She knew that Ivor had given money to Brownlow to pay the hairdresser, but was horrified to learn how much he charged.

"He be the very best in Mayfair, Your Highness," Brownlow explained. "It were only by tellin' him you had a title that he agreed to come to you tonight."

"I only hope I do him credit," Weena sighed.

She need not have worried.

It was with a certain apprehension that she walked up the steps of the grand house in Pall Mall the carriage took them to.

There was a red carpet to walk on and oil lamps to reveal the steps up to the front door.

The footman, who had opened their carriage door, was wearing an elaborate and intricate uniform.

As soon as they entered the house, she just knew at once that its owners must be very important and very rich.

Lady Carstairs was receiving her guests in a room massed with flowers and lit with dozens of candles.

When their name was announced in stentorian tones by a butler who in many ways resembled Brownlow, Lady Carstairs gave a cry of delight and held out both hands to Ivor.

"I am so charmed to meet you, Your Highness. Our dear friend, Prince Feodor, would, I know be delighted that you are here with me."

"Both my sister and I are not only thrilled but very grateful for your kind welcome to London," Ivor replied.

He was looking exceedingly smart as he always did in his evening clothes.

Weena realised that there was a glint in the eyes of every woman who looked at him.

Now, as he bent over to kiss his hostess's hand, she realised without being told by anyone that her dear brother, Ivor, would undoubtedly be a huge success in the London Society.

If she was also one as well, it would be entirely due to his cleverness and most of all to the titles he had given them.

CHAPTER SIX

After dinner, during which Weena had sat next to two rather elderly and not particularly interesting men, they moved into the music room where they were to dance.

She was instantly pursued by a number of young gentlemen who were smartly dressed and obviously excited by the idea of someone new.

She accepted the first one who asked her to dance.

As he took her round the ballroom to the tune of a dreamy waltz, he said,

"You are very lovely and look very different from the English girls. I am sure you will be the belle of the ball at every ball you attend."

Weena smiled.

"That is just what my brother who brought me here hopes. But, of course, I am much too modest to think of anything like that."

The man she was dancing with laughed.

"Tell me about Russia," he suggested. "It's a place I have never visited, but have often thought that it would be interesting to do so."

"Where we lived," Weena answered him, "is very quiet and in the depths of the country. But I am sure that you would enjoy St. Petersburg and all the parties that are given there."

"I think perhaps that I would be more amused with you in the country," he replied, "especially if your horses are good."

"I can answer you truthfully, they are just superb," Weena asserted. "The one reason I hated coming away is because I have had to leave my horses behind."

"If you feel like that I am sure that I will see you in Rotten Row tomorrow morning," her partner smiled.

"It depends on if my brother can find horses that he thinks are good enough for us."

He laughed.

"I can assure you in London we have the best that are available and, as I have just said, I will be looking for you tomorrow morning."

She danced every dance and every partner without exception congratulated her on her looks.

They all said that they were interested in Russia although none of them had ever been there.

It was much later in the evening that the Prince of Wales arrived.

Lady Carstairs hurried forward clearly delighted at his appearance.

"I promised I would come if I could get away from my boring dinner party," the Prince of Wales said. "Now show me all the beautiful girls. A dance will certainly be a change from the long and gloomy speeches I have had to endure for the last three hours."

Lady Carstairs then looked round the room and saw that Weena was not far away.

"Come and meet the very latest visitor to Mayfair," she trumpeted. "Her brother, Prince Ivor, was a friend of our beloved Prince Feodor. As they have only just arrived, he and his sister are new faces for us to admire and talk to."

The Prince of Wales chortled.

Weena, who had only just finished dancing, looked round in surprise as they approached her.

"His Royal Highness," Lady Carstairs began, "was saying very charming things about our dear Prince Feodor who we miss so very much."

It took a second or so for Weena to realise that the Prince of Wales was standing in front of her.

Then, as she swept to the ground in a deep curtsey, the Prince suggested,

"As I have been deprived of beautiful ladies all this evening, I hope you will dance with me to make up for the time I have missed at this delightful party!"

Only as he swung her around the room did Weena realise that all the girls present were looking at her with envy.

She was not aware that the Prince of Wales seldom paid any attention to young women. He liked them older and usually married.

After the Prince of Wales's arrival, the dance floor was crowded with guests who wished to gaze at him and if possible attract his attention.

"Tell me why you are here?" he asked Weena.

"It was my brother, Ivor, who wanted to come to England, Your Royal Highness. As our parents are now dead, he reckoned that I was wasting my time just sitting under the trees in the Caucasus."

The Prince of Wales guffawed.

"Of course your brother is quite right. We are the lucky ones to benefit from Russia's loss!"

Weena thought him delightful and more than kind to her.

She did not realise what a disturbance she had just caused until going home in the carriage when Ivor piped up,

"If I had planned it myself, it could not have been a better *entrée* into London Society."

"You mean dancing with the Prince of Wales?"

"Of course I mean it. Do you realise that he never dances with *debutantes* or young girls? And his love affairs are always with older beauties who are usually married or widowed."

"I thought that he was very charming," Weena said, "and I am glad for your sake that I was a success."

"For both our sakes. Don't forget you have to be married and, as my wife, when I find her, will obviously not want to keep you for long in the manner I want you to shine at, but have not had the chance until now?"

Weena did not answer as she hated to think that she would be married hastily to someone she did not love.

When she retired to bed, she found herself thinking and longing for David Hart.

'How could he have possibly gone without saying goodbye to me?' she asked herself again as she had already asked a million times. 'I wanted to tell him that when he returns to England he must come and see us wherever we might be. But obviously – he was not interested.'

When she thought about all the young men she had danced with this evening, she knew that, smart and dashing though they might seem, they did not do the strange things to her heart which had happened when she had been with David.

'It's no use my loving him – ' she mused.

At the same time she fell asleep thinking of him and he was her first thought when she awoke the following morning.

*

When she went down to breakfast, her brother had already made plans as to what they should do that day.

"The first thing," he said, "is that I must have more money. I managed to find out last night from one of the older members of the party that the man who is most likely to help me is called Simpson, who has a very large antique shop in Bond Street."

Weena was listening intently and he went on,

"Apparently he is well known both in England and on the Continent. Those who want particular pictures or a unique piece of furniture always consult him."

"And you have plenty of them!" Weena exclaimed.

"I know and the sooner I can begin selling them the better. One thing no one expects or appreciates in London is people who don't pay their bills and then cannot give the sort of parties like the one we attended last night."

"Would it cost so very much to throw a big party?" Weena asked Ivor seriously.

"Of course it would," he answered her impatiently. "The band is not cheap and we were drinking the very best champagne at dinner and afterwards which needless to say is not given away with a pound of tea!"

Weena was now looking worried.

But before she could speak, he continued,

"We need horses and, of course, I would like to buy my own rather than hire them."

He paused for a moment before he added,

"I have learnt that everyone expects the Russians to be extravagant simply because the tales of the Palaces and parties at St. Petersburg lose nothing in the telling."

"You are frightening me again," Weena replied.

Ivor smiled.

"If we can obtain good prices for our pictures and all the other items we have brought with us, the money will last, as I have already said, until you find a husband and I a wife for myself."

Weena wanted to say outright that she did not want to be married, but knew it would only annoy her brother.

So she said nothing and went upstairs quickly after breakfast to put on her hat so that she could go with him to Mr. Simpson's shop in Bond Street.

By the time she came downstairs, he had ordered a carriage which was outside.

He was waiting for the servants to bring him one or two of the pictures that had been placed in the Gallery where he intended, once they were framed, to hang them.

When he told Weena what he was doing, she said,

"I think that this is a mistake. You should talk to Mr. Simpson first and ask him to come to you rather than you go to him with what you have to sell."

Her brother looked at her at first in surprise.

Then he gave a loud exclamation.

"You are quite right! Of course the man must come to me and I should behave in all ways as a grandee. In fact I will pretend at first that I am a buyer rather than a seller."

"I am sure that is best," Weena said. "I remember when Papa was visiting a shop that contained anything he was interested in to add to his collection, they bowed again and again to him. They were so excited by his appearance that I used to laugh and tell Papa that they stumbled over their words as well as over their feet!"

"That is what they must do to me," Ivor said. "It was very stupid of me not to think of it myself."

"I am quite certain that if you want to get a really good price for anything you have," Weena said, "you have to pretend that you are selling it reluctantly rather than that you are eager to do so."

"I know exactly how I shall behave now you have told me. I cannot think why I was so stupid as not to have thought it out myself."

They drove off in the carriage.

Then Ivor said,

"You were a great success last night, Weena. I am quite sure by the time we go home there will be a number of invitations for us from other hostesses. In fact at least three of them told me last night that they will be sending us an invitation and that was well before you danced with the Prince of Wales!"

"It was certainly lucky for me that he did so. I had hoped that I would catch a glimpse of him while we were in London, but never in my wildest dreams did I think that I would be privileged enough to dance with him."

"But you did and everyone was surprised because he pays no attention to *debutantes* or young girls. If one thing is certain, it is that we will not have to pay for our dinner for the next few weeks!"

Weena laughed as he had meant her to do.

"If I was a success then I am sure you were too, Ivor."

"I sat next to a very attractive young girl at dinner," he replied. "Obviously I could not ask too many questions, but I found out that her name is Mavis Campbell. I think that her father is a Lord although I am not certain."

"Is she pretty?" Weena asked.

"She was not only beautiful but she had a way of saying things that were witty and I found her enchanting. But unfortunately, as there were so many at the party, I only managed to dance with her twice."

"I expect you will meet her again. You can look for her at the next few parties."

She wondered as she spoke if she had any chance of meeting David in the same way.

Maybe he was not smart enough to go to the parties like the one last night and so she was not likely to run into him as she hoped to do.

It did not take them long to reach the shop in Bond Street.

Weena noticed at once that there was a very grand and fashionable carriage waiting outside.

It was drawn by two perfectly matched grey horses and the coachman and the footman were in very elaborate uniforms.

She thought that their employer must be Royalty or at least a gentleman of great riches.

They entered the shop which was very large and the walls were filled with many excellent pictures from floor to ceiling.

Besides tables on which were displayed all sorts of delightful pieces of china, there was a collection of snuff boxes that rivalled those Ivor had brought from their home.

As they went into the shop, a young man who was obviously an assistant bowed politely and said,

"The Proprietor is, at the moment, showing some pictures which have just arrived, to a gentleman. But I am certain that he will not be long before he attends to you. If you would like to walk round, sir, I will tell him that you are here. May I please have your name?"

"My name is Prince Ivor Kerlensky," Ivor said in a lofty manner. "As you have suggested, my sister and I will look round while we are waiting."

Everything in the shop was clearly worth looking at, but Weena was convinced that it was all very expensive.

They were both viewing a picture by Van Dyck that was undoubtedly in a very good condition when there was the sound of voices.

A man who was clearly the Proprietor accompanied by an older man and a young woman were walking along the passage and into the main part of the shop.

As they did so Ivor gave an exclamation and moved towards them.

He held out his hand to the girl walking behind the older man and said,

"I have been thinking about you and cursing myself in being so stupid as not to ask you for your address."

The girl gave a little laugh and replied,

"It's very nice to see you again. I would like you to meet my father, Lord Campbell."

The older man held out his hand.

"My daughter has been telling me that she met you at a recent party and your sister created a sensation when she danced with the Prince of Wales. May I say that I am delighted to meet both you and your sister?"

He shook hands with Ivor and then held out his hand to Weena.

As he did so, she was looking at the young girl and thinking that her brother was undoubtedly right.

She was certainly very beautiful and different in a way from the other girls who had been present at the party yesterday evening.

"I have heard," Lord Campbell was saying, "that Russia has more treasures than any country in Europe. So I cannot believe that you have come here as a purchaser as I have."

"What is your Lordship buying?" Ivor asked, "if it is not a personal question."

"It is one I am delighted to answer," Lord Campbell replied. "In fact I am always trying to add more to my various collections."

He turned to the Proprietor and went on,

"He has found me a Titian which I am thrilled to obtain."

Ivor gave an exclamation.

"That is strange," he said, "because I have two in my collection as I was coming here to ask the Proprietor where I can best have them framed. As you can imagine, I brought a number of pictures with me, but without frames, as that would have made them heavy and cumbersome."

Lord Campbell stared at him.

"Are you saying that you have several pictures by Titian?"

Ivor nodded.

"If you are collecting Titians, my Lord, then you must certainly come and see mine. I think it is some of his early work, but all the same they are excellent examples of the Master's art, even though I say so myself."

"Of course I would like to see them," he replied.

"Then I will be pleased to show them to you, my Lord. At the same time they are not looking their best nor is anything else that I have brought with me which is quite a collection, simply because we have only just arrived in London and the house I have rented is full of dust. It will take some time to clean it up."

"That would not worry me," Lord Campbell said. "So please be very kind and let me see your pictures before anyone else tries to grab them away from you."

"I had not thought of selling them," Ivor responded. "But, as we cannot return to our home, I brought away with me everything that was easily portable."

"Why can you not return?" Lord Campbell asked.

Ivor gave a deep sigh.

"I think you would know the answer to that, my Lord. It was a question of saving the most precious things I possessed or having them taken away from me and, as far as we were concerned, being burnt to the ground."

Lord Campbell gave an exclamation,

"I have heard what is happening in Russia but could not believe it to be true."

"Unfortunately it is," Ivor replied, "and it will, of course, increase year after year. My sister and I, who are orphans, thought that it was wise to move while we could. But some of the objects we cherished had to be left behind and I regret to say that we will never see them again."

"It is certainly a sad story," Lord Campbell said. "But please let me see your collection and advise you what to keep and what to part with."

Lord Campbell was clever enough, Weena thought, who was listening, to realise that they would contemplate parting with their possessions sooner or later.

She was not surprised when her brother suggested,

"Supposing, my Lord, you and your daughter have tea with us today. I expect you are going out this evening and I have a feeling that we might be doing the same. But if you don't mind a certain amount of dust and discomfort, you will be the first to see what I have brought with me from Russia and advise me where I can go and have my pictures framed which is actually what I came to this shop for."

Lord Campbell grinned.

"You cannot do better than to trust Simpson. If you do have something to sell in the future, I would like to be your first customer before Simpson sells it on for a good profit to his customers, who are always pleading for what they think is a snip."

Both men laughed at this.

Mr. Simpson who had been listening smiled wanly.

It was as if he now realised that as things were Lord Campbell could take away the cream of what was available while he was left with the worst.

Lord Campbell then walked towards the door.

Mavis held out her hand to Ivor.

"I will look forward to seeing you this afternoon," she said.

"And I will be counting the minutes until I see you," he replied.

For a moment he held her hand in both of his.

Then, as she glanced up into his eyes, she blushed and, turning round, hurried after her father.

As the Proprietor bowed them out, Ivor whispered,

"That was a bit of luck."

From the way that he spoke, Weena did not know whether he was speaking of meeting up with the beautiful Mavis again or interesting her father in his pictures.

The Proprietor came back.

"Lord Campbell sounds as though he is a very big collector," Ivor said.

"He is indeed, Your Highness," Mr. Simpson then replied. "But he can well afford it seeing how rich he is."

"Is he rich?" Ivor asked.

He spoke coolly as if he was not that interested.

But Weena held her breath as Mr. Simpson replied,

"They say he is the richest man in England. Made a fortune in shipping he has."

Ivor did not answer.

He merely began to talk about the array of pictures in the shop.

He also asked to see the frames he wanted for his pictures and how much they would cost.

Weena was not listening.

She was thinking that her brother had found the rich girl he was seeking even quicker than she had expected.

He had found her very attractive last night and what more could he want than to be married to – if Mr. Simpson was to be believed – the daughter of the richest man in England.

'It just cannot be true,' she thought. 'And yet if it is, my prayers have been answered and we are even luckier than we hoped to be."

She was thinking exactly the same when, after they had finished tea, they went up into the Gallery where Ivor had planned to hang his pictures.

They had gone home after they had inspected the outstanding collection of pictures and endless *objects d'art* that Mr. Simpson had on display in his shop.

Ivor had unpacked the pictures and arranged them on the tables and chairs in what they believed had once been a Picture Gallery.

It was impossible to hang them without frames, but the way he had arranged them made them look attractive and intriguing.

Weena was not surprised when Lord Campbell was impressed.

"You have a fortune here, my boy," he said to Ivor "and, if you have to sell them, don't be taken for a mug."

"I have no wish to be," Ivor replied. "You must understand that, as we could not bring anything more than we have with us, this is my entire capital, which will have to last my sister and me for a very long time."

"One thing I would like you to promise me," Lord Campbell said, "is that, if you do decide to sell, which I am certain that you will sooner or later, you give me the first opportunity to buy."

There was silence for a moment.

Then Ivor said,

"Well, in point of fact, I was not thinking of selling anything yet, my Lord, as we have quite enough to live on for a little while, I think it is only fair that my sister should enjoy herself at the parties we are invited to. Of course she will want pretty dresses to wear and we both need good horses to ride."

It was then that Lord Campbell began to discuss with Ivor the price of two of the pictures he particularly wanted to add to his collection.

Weena now thought that Ivor was being particularly clever to appear reluctant to part with anything.

She and Mavis then went into another room where a number of letters had just arrived.

Weena guessed that they were the invitations which had been promised them last night by some of the guests of Lady Carstairs who had told Ivor how fond they were of Prince Feodor.

While she opened them, Mavis told her what she knew about the hostesses who had invited them.

"Here is one for tonight," Weena said. "Will you be there, Mavis?"

"Yes, I am sure that is where we are going and I will look forward to dancing with your brother again."

"He was afraid that he would not see you again," Weena remarked, "because he had been silly enough not to ask for your address."

Mavis laughed.

"Why does he want such a large house, if there is only you and him?" she asked.

Mavis had already said that her mother was dead and her father wanted to buy a house in the country as the one they had previously lived in was too small for him.

Mavis laughed and continued,

"Papa likes everything he owns to be bigger than anyone else's. When you see the vast number of books and pieces of china he has collected we really need a place as huge as Buckingham Palace to put them all in! And Ivor is just the same."

The two girls giggled.

Weena was then aware that she liked Mavis.

And if her brother had to marry anyone, she would welcome Mavis if that was his choice because there was something about her which made Weena feel that she was genuine in every way.

She could not explain it exactly to herself, but she had known many people in Russia who had made her feel, although she could not exactly explain why, that they were not entirely truthful.

She expected that those in the Social world would be somewhat unreal or maybe deceptive because they were acting out a part on a grand stage.

When later the men re-joined them, Weena knew without him having to say so, that Ivor had struck a good bargain with Lord Campbell and from his point of view it was all very satisfactory.

Lord Campbell then gave them both an invitation to have luncheon with him tomorrow.

"I expect," he said, "we will be going to some party or another in the evening. While I often think I would like to stay at home and enjoy my pictures, I have to remember that my daughter is young and she must have a choice of all the eligible young men in London before she decides to settle down and be married."

"I am sure she will have no difficulty about that, my Lord," Ivor said.

There was, however, a note in his voice and a light in his eyes that told his sister that, if anyone was to possess the attractive Mavis, he intended that it should be him.

When they said goodbye and left, Weena showed her brother the list of invitations they had already received.

Two more had arrived while they were having tea.

"You are a success, a huge success!" Ivor told his sister. "All we have to do now is find you a husband."

"There is no hurry," Weena countered quickly.

"Well, I know who I am going to marry and you are not allowed three guesses!"

"I think you are right, she is enchanting," his sister replied, "at the same time you do think that you will love her despite her money?"

"I thought when I first saw her," Ivor replied, "that she was the most attractive girl I have ever seen. Strange though it may seem, my heart turned a somersault."

Weena gave a little cry.

"Oh, Ivor, I am so happy if that is true! I was afraid that you may have to marry someone who was either very dull or perhaps unpleasant simply because she was rich. I like Mavis and I would like her even if she did not have a penny."

"I would like to say the same, but that would make it very difficult. As it is, if things work out the way they are moving at the moment, I will be a very fortunate man."

"Of course you will," Weena agreed. "I do so want you to be happy."

"Just as I want you to be happy, my lovely sister. So we have to start looking for someone who will give you everything you want in life."

Weena did not answer.

She was in fact wondering once again as she had wondered so often already why exactly David Hart had not said goodbye to her.

*

They went to a party that evening, which was not as amusing or as glamorous as the party had been the night before.

Ivor was upset when he found that Mavis was not there when they arrived and she did not even turn up when dinner was finished and the band started to play.

It was a disappointing party.

And Weena found one man rather tiresome.

She sat next to him at dinner and discovered that he was a certain Viscount Pendleton who lived in the North of England.

He had come to London as his sister had asked him to give a dance for her daughter, who was just eighteen.

As head of a well known family, he was, Weena thought, very stuck-up in many ways.

He was, in fact, determined to establish himself as a man of importance and she was, however, certain that there were many men there of far greater consequence than he was.

He talked to her in a lofty way at dinner trying, she thought, to impress her with his large estate and his family in general.

Although to be honest, she did think that perhaps he was trying to equal the position she held as a Princess.

As it was, she kept forgetting that this title gave her privileges that other *debutantes* did not have.

She sat at the top table at dinner for instance.

On one side of her was the Viscount, while on the other was a good-looking young man who was intent on being involved in politics before, as he swiftly pointed out, he was obliged to move to the House of Lords.

She found dinner with both of them rather boring particularly as the Viscount was completely determined to hold her attention regardless of how many others wanted to talk to her.

When the band started to play he asked her to dance before anyone else could do so and so she was obliged to accept him.

Although she tried to avoid him later, he somehow managed to make it impossible for her to refuse to dance with him again.

They had at least five dances before Ivor wanted to go home and then Weena was only too willing to agree with him.

Driving back to the house, he said,

"I could see that Viscount Pendleton was running after you. I have discovered that he is very well-off and owns a fine castle in the North and excellent racehorses that are kept at Newmarket."

"I thought him a bore," Weena replied. "He only talked about himself and he did not dance nearly as well as the other gentlemen."

"All the same he is rich," Ivor repeated, "and, if he asks us to stay at his castle, we will most certainly accept the invitation."

Weena thought that that was one thing she had no wish to do, but decided it best not to say so.

She began to talk about where they were going the following evening and if they were really going to ride in Rotten Row the next morning.

"I have asked for two horses to be brought round at a quarter-to-eight," Ivor told her. "The man has promised me that they are his very best ones and they are certainly the most expensive."

Weena gave a little cry.

"Oh, do be careful! If we spend too much money then we will have to keep selling more of your precious collection of treasures and they will not last for ever."

"I am well aware of that," Ivor replied. "I have my plans for the future and I will not give you any more than three guesses as to what they are."

"I don't want three. I think you are in love with Mavis and as she is so attractive I do hope that, if you have to marry, you will marry her."

"I hope so too," her brother agreed. "All the same it's not going to be easy. It depends on whether a Russian Prince is as important as an English Duke in the eyes of her father."

"Well, I can cheer you up," Weena said, "by saying that so far we have not met a Duke. As you are the man on the spot, I would think that Lord Campbell is wise enough to think 'a bird in the hand is worth two in the bush'."

Ivor laughed.

But Weena had the feeling that what she said was the truth and if he really wanted to marry Mavis, he might be successful.

Their ride in Rotten Row was a great success.

The moment she arrived there was a circle of young gentlemen around Weena and, when she trotted down the Row itself, they were beside and behind her.

She saw a number of girls who were also riding look at her angrily, but she told herself it was only because she was someone new.

Once they were used to her, there would be another newcomer or perhaps they would become bored.

It was Ivor who suggested that she must buy some more clothes because it would be unfashionable to appear in the same dress too often.

As they were asked out to dinner or a party almost every night, she thought that he was undoubtedly right.

So she indulged herself in a really beautiful dress, which had, the *couturier* assured her, come straight from Paris.

She was certainly a success in it that evening and, in spite of the fact that she was being pestered by Viscount Pendleton again, she enjoyed every moment.

"I insist on you calling me by my Christian name," he said, "and, in case you have forgotten, it is 'Randolph'."

Weena wanted to tell him that she once had a dog called that name, but thought he would not have found it amusing.

He was continually puffed up with his own self-importance and, although she tried to stop him, he wrote his name down half a dozen times on her dance card.

"There are lots of other girls you should dance with because they are your friends," she told him.

"I want to dance with you," he replied brusquely.

There was a look in his eyes that frightened her and she tried to move away, but he took her almost physically onto the dance floor.

"You *must* dance with me!" he persisted. "And you dance far better than any woman I have ever danced with. As you are much more beautiful than they are, why should I dance with anyone but you?"

She knew that there was no point in arguing with him and so she danced with him until the waltz came to an end.

Then she almost ran to the partner whose name was on her card for the next dance.

It was when this one was over that Weena, dancing round the room, saw that the Viscount had disappeared.

She hoped he had gone home and would therefore not claim the other dances he had written down on her card despite her protests.

"Let's go into the garden now," she said, because she was anxious to hide from the Viscount.

Her partner agreed all too eagerly.

Once outside in the garden, he tried to kiss her but was rather clumsy about it.

It was easy for her to refuse him, but it might not have been so easy with anyone else.

However, she thought it would be wise to return to the ballroom even though she might have to dance with the Viscount again.

It was still early in the evening and more guests were continually arriving.

She looked round for her brother, but could not see him anywhere.

Then to her surprise a servant came to her side.

"His Highness, the Prince, requests Your Highness to join him in the upstairs sitting room," he told her.

Weena looked at him in surprise.

"I will now show Your Highness where it is," the servant offered.

There was nothing she could do but follow him up the stairs.

They had been dancing on the ground floor and she had only been up the stairs to put her cloak down and tidy herself before dinner.

Now the servant in front of her opened one of the doors on the first floor.

As she entered, she saw that it was a private sitting room. It had a pine bookcase on one side of the room and a secretaire by the window.

As she entered, she saw, sitting on the sofa by the fireplace that were two men, her brother and the Viscount.

They both rose as she came into the room.

As the door closed behind her, she wondered why Ivor had sent for her in such a peremptory manner.

She walked towards him and Ivor put out his hands and took hers.

"My dearest," he began. "I have some good news for you. I am very happy to tell you that his Lordship, the Viscount Pendleton, has asked for your hand in marriage. And it is with the greatest pleasure I have told him on your behalf that you will be his wife!"

For a moment Weena just stared at her brother in sheer astonishment.

Then, as she saw the expression on the Viscount's rather ugly face and the glint in his eyes, she felt the whole horror of the prospect sweep over her.

With a cry that seemed to almost echo round the room, she pulled her hand away from her brother's and ran towards the door.

As she pulled it open, she heard Ivor calling after her,

"Weena, don't be so ridiculous! Come back here!"

She ran out of the room, slamming the door behind her.

As she reached the stairs, she started to run down them frantically.

She had no idea where she was going.

She only knew that it was impossible and she could not marry the Viscount. But she was afraid, desperately afraid, that her brother would force her.

As she was halfway down the staircase, a servant was just opening the front door and a man came in.

He was wearing evening clothes and he took off his top hat to hand it to one of the footmen in attendance.

When she could see him more clearly in the light from the candles, Weena realised who he was.

As she reached the last three stairs she ran down them.

Realising exactly who the newcomer was, she flung herself against him.

"*David*! David!" she cried. "*Save me*! Save me!"

CHAPTER SEVEN

For a moment David stiffened as if he could hardly believe what was happening.

Then he put his arms round her and took her out through the front door which was not quite closed.

There was a smart carriage outside and a footman, who had obviously just opened the door for the occupant, was now climbing back on to his seat beside the coachman.

"Stop!" David shouted.

As the coachman pulled at the horses who were just beginning to move, the footman jumped down and opened the door of the carriage.

Weena was still clinging to David.

He picked her up in his arms and put her into the carriage.

Then he climbed in beside her.

As the footman waited for orders, David called out,

"Carter, first drive slowly through Hyde Park and then go back home."

The footman closed the door and climbed up to his seat and the horses set off.

It was then that Weena, who had been hiding her face on David's shoulder, cried,

"How could you be here just when I wanted you? I thought I would never see you again, David. Oh, *David*!"

"I have been cursing myself endlessly for leaving you on the ship without finding out where you would be staying in London," David replied.

"I missed you, I missed you so so much," Weena whispered.

"As I missed you," David answered.

He had one arm round her and now he very gently raised her face from his shoulder.

"You are so lovely and so beautiful," he murmured. "How could I have been such a fool as to let you go?"

He did not wait for an answer as his lips found hers.

As he kissed her, Weena knew in her heart that this was what she had been waiting for and longing for.

She loved him not only with her body but with her soul.

David kissed her for what seemed a long time.

Then, holding her closely in his arms, he said,

"Forgive me! Forgive me for being so stupid and leaving you as I did. I have suffered every moment of the day and night since I let you go."

"And I thought only of you," Weena sighed.

"Now tell me what has upset you, my darling," he asked. "From what do I have to save you this time?"

"From marrying a man who Ivor has chosen for me because he is rich and important. He is horrible and I hate him."

"If you are going to marry anyone," David told her positively, "it will be *me*. I know now that I cannot live without you, Weena, and I need you as I have never needed anyone in my whole life before."

Weena was very still.

Then she stammered in a voice that did not sound like her own,

"Are you *really* – asking me to – marry you?"

"I am, and I mean to marry you," David answered. "I ran away because I thought that the idea would shock and upset my family. It was only when I realised I might never see you again that I knew I had been a complete and utter fool and I could not live without you."

"Oh, David, I thought too that I would never see you again. I have prayed and prayed every night that I might find you and now you have come at exactly the right time to save me from that horrible, horrible man."

"You feel like that yet your brother still wants you to marry him?" David asked.

"Ivor said that we both had to marry someone with money because the family treasures we have brought from Russia will not last for ever. But he has found someone he loves and who I am sure loves him."

"Then, of course, they will be happy when they are married," David asserted, "just as *we* will be even happier when we are married, my darling, because you love me and I love you."

As if he could not help himself, he kissed her again, at first gently and then more passionately.

He felt her respond and she moved even closer to him than she was already.

"I cannot believe this is happening," she sighed. "I have thought of you so much and wondered how you could leave me without even saying goodbye."

"I was a fool," David replied. "I listened to my family telling me over and over again how I must marry someone and produce an heir. I had mothers of *debutantes* practically throwing them into my arms. So I thought – "

He paused.

"You will have to forgive me, my darling, for what I thought, but I must tell you the truth."

"What – is it?" Weena asked him hesitantly.

"I thought you were not grand enough to please my family. Therefore, because I wanted you so desperately, I ran away."

"I still don't understand you," Weena replied, "how your family, who have never met me, could disapprove of anyone you wanted to marry."

David gave a little laugh.

"I suppose rather like your brother wants money, they want someone of Social significance."

Weena was silent for a moment.

Then she asked,

"Why should they want that?"

"That is why, my darling, I was travelling under a false name."

Weena gave a little cry.

"I did not think of that. When you left, I thought that you were no longer interested in me. I felt certain that, even if you had stayed as you were on such a cheap ship, Ivor would have said that you were not rich enough."

"But you were a guest at a very grand Social party tonight," David said, "wearing such a lovely gown that I would not have expected you to own when we were on the ship together."

"It's a long story," Weena murmured. "I will tell you everything soon. Now I can only feel as if you have just dropped down from Heaven when I was crying out for you."

"This will not happen again," he promised. "You are going to marry me whatever your brother or my family may say."

"I cannot imagine anything more wonderful – than being married to you," Weena whispered. "When I missed you so terribly, I found that every man I met was so dull and uninteresting because he was not you."

David smiled.

"I might easily say the same thing. I kept thinking that I would see you again when I reached London, then I remembered that I had no address for you. I asked at the Russian Embassy if they had ever heard of a Miss Alweena Dawson, but they assured me that they had no one of that name on their books."

Weena laughed.

"Of course you could not know that we assumed that name simply because Ivor did not wish to spend a lot of money travelling and he was certain that the treasures we brought with us from our home would only last perhaps a year."

"So you really are refugees?" David asked.

"Yes, we are, but now everyone is making a fuss of us in London and we are asked to numerous parties. And Ivor has suddenly decided that I will marry this horrible man because he is a Viscount and rich."

"Where were you going just now?" David asked.

"I suppose I shall have to go back to the house we have rented," Weena replied. "So you will have to take me there please."

"I will take you there as soon as you promise me that you will not run away again and hide so that I lose you."

"I will never do that," Weena assured him. "But we may have a struggle on our hands with Ivor because he is determined that I will marry this Viscount."

David smiled.

"I reckon that I can persuade your brother that I am a better husband for you than a mere Viscount!"

"If the worst comes to the worst we will have to run away," Weena said, as if she was thinking it all out. "If we get married secretly, then no one could ever take me away from you."

"I have no intention of making a secret of the fact that you are the most beautiful girl I have ever seen. And, as I love you and you love me, no one and nothing will prevent us from being married."

Weena gave a little sigh of contentment and put her head down on his shoulder.

"It was so like you to save me when I was very frightened and it's the third time you have done so," she exclaimed.

"Three times lucky. I think I had better take you back to where you are staying and then we will face your brother and, if necessary, the Viscount tomorrow."

"I don't want to leave you," Weena whispered.

"And I want to stay all night kissing you," David murmured. "But I am thinking of you, my precious, and I cannot have you all tired and exhausted tomorrow when I meet with your brother and fight a battle for you which I am determined to win."

Because she could not help herself, Weena laughed.

"You are making it sound exactly like a story in a book," she said. "Of course you will win the battle and we will live happily ever afterwards."

"That is what I am quite certain we will do," David replied. "But now I am going to take you home. It's late and I was only dropping in on the party where I found you simply to apologise for not being able to be there earlier as I promised to be."

Weena wanted to say that she wished she could stay with him for the rest of the night.

But she knew there might be a fuss if her brother thought that she had been out so long with David, whose friendship Ivor had most definitely not encouraged.

In fact, when David had disappeared at Lisbon, he had said,

"That man you are always talking to has now gone ashore and a good job too if you ask me. It's no use you getting yourself interested in a poor man when you know as well as I do that we have to seek out millionaires."

He had spoken somewhat disagreeably and she had not answered him, as she knew that it was no use having a row over David when he was no longer on board.

Now she thought if David was going to the party she had just left, then he was clearly of more consequence than they had thought him to be.

Perhaps her brother would be a little more pleasant to him than he had been on board ship.

Equally she knew despairingly that, whatever she said or whatever she did, he would still want her to marry the dreadful Viscount Pendleton.

Moving a little nearer to David, she said,

"Listen David! Can we get married very quickly without anyone knowing about it? So then, whatever Ivor might say, it would be too late to alter anything."

David's arms tightened around her.

"Darling, are you still thinking that I am as poor as I appeared to be on board that ship?"

"Well, I suppose you must be staying with people who lent you this smart carriage," Weena said, "but that would not make you rich enough in Ivor's eyes."

"You can leave your brother to me," David assured her. "But I just want to ask you one question, my darling, which I want you to answer truthfully."

"What is – that?" Weena enquired.

"Would you still marry me if I really was poor and unimportant regardless of what your brother says?"

"I would marry you if you were just a crossing-sweeper!" Weena answered. "If we are poor, I promise I will look after you and I can cook rather well actually."

David laughed.

"I am sure that you do everything wonderfully and no one could look as beautiful as you. I have never seen you before arrayed in so much finery."

"It's a long and complicated story and I will tell you all about it tomorrow," Weena said.

She was suddenly afraid that if David was as poor as he had appeared to be that Ivor would be furious at her marrying him.

Perhaps, whatever David might say, they might still have to run away.

As if he knew exactly what she was thinking, David sighed,

"I think, my precious one, the only thing that really matters is that we love each other. Nothing else is of the least consequence."

"I love you, I adore you," Weena told him. "If I have to scrub floors and cook in a tiny cottage, as long as I am with you I will be really, really happy, I promise you."

She could not say anymore because David was now kissing her again and she felt as if she was melting into him and was a part of him.

All the angels were singing in Heaven and she was touching the stars

David then asked her where she was staying.

When she gave him the address, for a moment he looked surprised.

Then he said,

"I suppose you are staying with friends and Park Lane is the right place for you. But then you would look lovely wherever you are. Either in the smallest cottage, as you have already said, or in a Palace."

"I would be quite happy, David, as long as I was with you."

He kissed her again as if no words could tell her how much he loved her.

He was still kissing her when they stopped outside the house in Park Lane.

"Now go straight to bed," David suggested. "I will call and see you after breakfast tomorrow. So do *not* start to fight with your brother until I arrive. I promise you if there is to be a fight, which I think unlikely, I will get my own way – and you."

He kissed her on the last word.

As the door of the carriage was opened, he stepped out first to help her to the ground.

He took her to the door and the night-footman, who had heard the carriage arrive, opened it before Weena had to knock.

"Goodnight, David," she whispered.

"Goodnight, darling" he said and, taking her hand, kissed it.

As he then turned away towards the carriage, the night-footman closed the door and she ran up the stairs.

As she expected Ivor was still not back.

She went into her own room.

Even before she took off her dress, she knelt down at the side of the bed and thanked God for sending David to her rescue yet again.

She prayed for quite a long time before she finally undressed and climbed into bed.

It was only when she had turned out the light and shut her eyes did she hear her brother coming upstairs.

He stopped for a moment outside her door as if to make sure that she was asleep.

Then he went on to his own room and she heard the door close.

Because she was so happy at finding David nothing else mattered.

When she fell asleep, her lips were smiling.

Now the future was golden and nothing else was of any interest because she and David were together.

*

The following morning she was late downstairs for breakfast.

She walked into the dining room feeling just a little nervous as to what Ivor would say to her.

"Good morning, Weena," he began as she entered the room. "I nearly came in to tell you last night my good news, but I thought it a mistake for you to be more tired than you were already. So I kept it until this morning."

"Good – news?" Weena questioned him anxiously.

"Mavis has promised to marry me and we are to have a large and impressive wedding in three weeks time."

Weena gave a little cry.

"Oh, Ivor, I am so glad. She is so pretty and I am sure that you will be very happy."

"I am in love with her," he said, "and she is in love with me. For the moment that seems even more important than her father's immense fortune."

Weena clapped her hands.

"That is exactly how you *should* feel."

She was just about to add that was how she felt too, but thought it was not the right time.

She therefore went on,

"I think she is very lovely and I am sure that she would marry you if you did not have a title and were of no standing Socially."

"I doubt if her father would let me marry her under those circumstances," Ivor said. "But, as it is, everything is perfect. The old man is giving us a house in London and already Mavis runs his house in the country. As her father is so often away in America and on the Continent, I will have to be in complete charge of all his affairs including running his racehorses."

Weena gave a cry of delight and clapped her hands together.

"That is perfect and exactly what you wanted. As you well know, as you have run our huge estate for Papa for the last five years, you will not have any difficulty in managing another."

"That is what I felt myself. Of course racehorses are what I have always longed to own and needless to say my future father-in-law has the best."

He spoke with such satisfaction that Weena could only think that he was a very lucky man.

'Even if I am not so lucky,' she thought to herself, 'I am marrying the man I love and nothing else counts.'

Ivor drank his coffee and then he said,

"Now we have to think about you, Weena. You ran away last night, but I told the Viscount that girls are often shy. He would have to woo you without upsetting you and it would perhaps be for the best if you are married before me."

Weena drew in her breath.

Then she said,

"I think perhaps we had better discuss this matter in another room as the servants will be coming in here with my breakfast at any moment and I don't want them to think that we are quarrelling."

"We are not going to quarrel," Ivor said. "I wish to have my own way in looking after you and you have to see sense and, of course, nothing could be more fortunate than that you should have a title and marry into a family which is acknowledged to be one of the oldest and most respected in England."

As Weena had no wish to argue with him, she was thankful when at that moment the door opened and then Brownlow came in with her breakfast.

"I've been keepin' it hot for Your Highness," he said, "and I think you'll enjoy it as the fish were fresh from the market this mornin'."

"I am sure it is delicious," Weena said, "and thank you, Brownlow, for remembering that I like sole more than any other fish."

"It were cook who remembered that," he replied as if he felt that he ought not to take all the credit.

Brownlow poured out a cup of coffee for Weena and then left the room.

Because she thought that David might be arriving at any moment, Weena hurried to eat her breakfast.

Before she had finished, her brother, picking up the newspapers that were lying on the side table, said,

"I want to talk to you and we will do it in the study. Join me as soon as you are ready and I expect that there will be a number of invitations to more parties and we will have to decide which are the best ones for us to accept."

He reached the door as he was speaking and went out closing it behind him.

Weena gave a sigh of relief.

She had no wish to quarrel with her brother or to upset him when he was so happy.

'He has everything he could possibly wish for,' she thought, 'and I want only one wish, which is David.'

They might be very poor, they might have to live in a small cottage in the country, but they would be together and nothing else could ever matter.

Perhaps if they saved up their money carefully they would occasionally be able to take a holiday.

He could show her some of the foreign places he had talked about and found so attractive.

It would not matter if they had to stay in very cheap lodgings as long as they were in each other's arms.

She would try in every way she could to make him feel that he was not in any way inferior to Ivor who now would have so much money and such valuable possessions.

She could not imagine Ivor being content with a cottage just because he was sharing it with Mavis.

'I would be happy in a cave if only David was with me,' she told herself again and again.

She felt once more the thrill of his kisses and the strange way her heart seemed to turn over when he told her that he loved her.

'I love him, I adore him,' she thought, 'and nothing must prevent us from being married.'

At the same time she was certain that Ivor intended to force her into marriage with the Viscount.

She would have to be very firm and resist him.

She could only hope that he would not be rude and unkind to David because he was of no importance as far as her brother was concerned.

She kept wondering to herself if he would have married Mavis if she had been as plain as a pikestaff.

But she would have fallen in love with Ivor anyway because he was so handsome and dashing.

She had seen the way that the women looked at him at parties.

She was very certain that when they thought of him as a romantic Prince, they were ready to surrender to his kisses.

Of course they would marry him if they had enough money for him to ask them to do so.

'I want to be married for myself,' Weena thought. 'And that is what David is doing. He saw us travelling in a very cheap ship and he loves me because I am me and not because I am pretending to be a Princess. Or in fact come from a decent Russian family even though the house and the estate is no longer ours.'

At the same time while she was so happy because David loved her just as she loved him, she realised that it was going to be a hard battle with her brother.

He was determined to cash in on the success she already was in the Social world and marry her to a future Earl.

'I hate the Viscount, I hate him!' she cried out to herself desperately.

But she knew it would not be the sort of argument her brother would listen to and she would have to think of something better.

It was then she had an idea and, jumping up from the breakfast table, ran into the hall.

"There is a gentleman calling to see me," she told Brownlow, who was instructing the new footman how to polish a side table.

"At what time does Your Highness expect him?" Brownlow asked.

"I don't know," Weena replied, "he just said that he would come here this morning. I will be in the study with His Highness."

"I'll bring him there when he arrives," Brownlow said. "Will you then be askin' the gentleman to stay on for luncheon?"

"I am not sure," Weena answered. "But tell cook we may be one extra and, of course, as usual we will be out to dinner tonight."

"I guessed that already, Your Highness."

As she walked away from him, Weena was thinking that perhaps she and David might have to run away.

In which case they would be out to dinner and have to find some small cheap place where they could eat.

It would be very different from the party that they had already accepted which was to take place that evening at the Duchess of Devonshire's house.

It would, Weena had already learnt, be one of the most prestigious balls of the Season.

Then, just as if she was being tempted, a voice in her mind piped up,

'Just think what you will miss if you are living in a small house in the country. No more dinner parties, no fast horses and you may never have a chance of wearing your pretty gowns like the one you are wearing this morning.'

As if Weena was listening to the voice and knew the answer, she said to herself,

'But I will be with David and that is what really matters.'

She reached the study door and entered to find Ivor sitting at the desk opening the letters that had arrived by the morning post.

"You will hardly believe it," he said in an excited voice as she came in. "But we have been asked to dine at Marlborough House!"

"Marlborough House?" she asked. "Who lives there?"

"Don't be so silly!" her brother snapped. "It's the Prince of Wales who has asked us or rather the Princess. Just think of it and only a short time ago we were watching those devils burn down our house and believing we were destitute and had nothing left in the world but what I had managed to hide away."

"It is certainly most exciting and a great honour to be asked to dine with the Prince of Wales," Weena agreed.

At the same time she was thinking that perhaps she would be unable to accept as she would have run away by then to the country with David.

"It will undoubtedly impress my future father-in-law," Ivor was saying. "He is so thrilled that his daughter is to be a Princess and has promised to pay an enormous sum of money into my bank account so that you need not worry about your trousseau. I promise you that it will be as beautiful and as expensive as Mavis's."

Weena did not answer for the simple reason that she knew it would be a mistake for her to go into battle with Ivor before David arrived.

Instead she picked up the newspapers that had been put on a stool in front of the fireplace and said,

"I am sure the party we attended last night will be reported in the Social columns and I want to see if we are mentioned."

"I have already done so," Ivor replied. "I assure you we are both there and they actually say that Princess Alweena was looking especially beautiful in a lovely dress of white tulle decorated with pink roses."

"Do they really say that or are you making it up?" Weena asked.

"Look for yourself," her brother told her, "and see how famous you are becoming. You are nearly at the top of the list of invited guests."

Weena had just found the piece about herself in *The Times* when the door opened and Brownlow announced,

"The Duke of Hartington, Your Highnesses."

Both Weena and Ivor looked towards the newcomer with surprise.

Then, as David walked into the room, Weena gave a little cry.

"David, it is *you!*" she called out.

He walked towards her.

Taking her hand, he kissed it before he said,

"We had so much to say to each other last night that I forgot to tell you who I am."

"But you were coming to London on the same ship with us!" Ivor now exclaimed.

"I was on the ship calling myself David Hart which is the name that I always use when I am travelling," David replied.

"But why did you bother to disguise yourself?" Ivor asked. "I don't understand."

"For much the same reason you were doing," David answered. "It was only just now when the butler asked my name that I realised you and Weena were still thinking of me as the man of no consequence you met on the ship."

"You were of great consequence to me," Weena murmured.

He took her hand and turned towards Ivor.

"I am sure," he said, "that you will not be surprised to learn that your sister and I want to be married as soon as possible."

Ivor then rose from the chair with his hand up to his forehead.

"I am now completely bewildered," he admitted. "I believed that we had disguised ourselves so as to travel as cheaply as possible, but I never for one moment thought that you might be doing the same."

"It is rather deflating to find that you and the people on board ship, who did not know my real name, thought I was of no standing whatsoever," David commented rather poignantly.

"But you were of great importance to me," Weena said again. "And you made me very happy until you ran away."

"I am ashamed for doing so," David replied. "It was only when I lost you that I realised it was impossible for me to live without you. I was determined to find you even if it took me a thousand years to do so."

Weena laughed.

"I am very glad it did not take you as long as that!"

"No, I was fortunate. When I went to the party last night, it was merely to apologise for being so late, but I found you and that mattered more than anything else."

He then gazed into her eyes as he spoke and it was impossible for either of them to look away.

And for a moment they forgot that Ivor was there in the room watching them.

In fact they both started when he broke the spell by saying,

"I still don't understand. If you are a Duke and I would imagine a very important one, why should you want to travel Second Class on that ship and in disguise?"

"Simply and solely because if you are a Duke," he replied, "you are pursued by very many people who are impressed only with your name and who wish to know you just because you have a prestigious title."

He pulled Weena a little nearer to him as he added,

"As you will find, a large number of people want to marry off their daughter to you because she can then share your title with you and thus impress her friends who are not so fortunate."

"But you did not tell me last night that you were a Duke," Weena pointed out.

"That is what makes the story even more wonderful for me than it is already," David replied. "I was always terrified of being married simply because of my title which is yet another reason why I hide it whenever I have the chance."

He paused for a moment before he said,

"But you, my darling one, promised to marry me without knowing who I actually am or for that matter what I possess."

"I would be extremely happy to be alone with you in a small cottage in the country," Weena whispered.

"I know," he answered. "That is what makes me even more grateful to the Gods who brought you to me in Greece. One of the things we will do on our honeymoon is to go back there and thank them for doing so."

"I would love that," Weena sighed. "It would be absolute Heaven to be in Greece with you."

"That is what I was thinking too," David added.

They gazed again into each other's eyes and forgot the world for a moment.

Then Ivor coughed and said,

"I am naturally delighted that my sister should be so happy. I can only suggest that, as I will want to give her away at what will obviously be a very lavish wedding, you should be married before Mavis and me. If our friends find it expensive having to provide two presents so quickly, I am not going to commiserate with them about it!"

They all laughed at this.

Then Ivor said,

"I know it is early in the morning, but we have to celebrate this unique occasion and I am going to ring for Brownlow to bring us a bottle of champagne."

"Anything will taste like the nectar of the Gods at this particular moment," David suggested.

He was quite certain later that the champagne had made it easy to persuade Ivor that they should be married as soon as possible.

"I want to take your sister on my new yacht," David said. "I am sure that she will need only a few days to buy her trousseau."

"I will mind dreadfully not being at your wedding, Ivor," Weena said, "but I do want to go away with David and see the places around the world he has told me about, which I thought I would only see in my dreams and read about in books."

"You will see them all," David insisted. "But it will not really matter what we are looking at. You know as well as I do it will be Heaven just to be with each other."

It seemed to Weena from that moment on that she could not think of anything except her wedding and the excitement of going away on their honeymoon.

She knew that every precious moment they were together she loved him more than she did already.

And she felt that he was telling her the truth when he said exactly the same.

*

It was only three days before they were actually to be married that Weena suddenly realised she had not told David, because it had not occurred to her, that she was not really a Princess and that she and Ivor had adopted the title simply to impress the English.

'I must tell him, I really must tell him,' she thought. 'How could I start my life with a lie? If he found out from anyone else, he would never forgive me.'

She thought about it all day when she was trying on clothes for her trousseau in the smart shops in Bond Street.

It was when she went to David's house in Belgrave Square that she knew she had to tell him the truth even if he would then no longer wish to marry her.

'I just cannot live a lie,' she told herself, 'and God would be angry and perhaps terrible things would happen simply because I was being wicked instead of good, as I was brought up to be.'

That night they were dining alone because instead of attending a party they were going to the ballet to see the beautiful dancing that David had told her about.

The ballet music was always so romantic and that is what they were both feeling as they held hands all the way through the performance.

Yet she was now afraid, deeply afraid that if she told him the truth he might cease to love her and disappear as he had done before.

She realised that one of the reasons he had never married was because he thought that women were attracted to him not for himself but for his title and possessions.

147

"I am told that every *debutante* wants to end up a Duchess," he had said scornfully. "So I was determined that I would never marry until someone really loved me for myself. That is what you have done, my darling. I knew then that I had found the true love I had always wanted. The love we both believe belongs to Greece and the Gods and Goddesses"

"Where you found me," Weena added softly.

"You fell down into my arms as if given to me by the Gods themselves," David said. "But I was too stupid not to realise that I had found what I was seeking and need never hide again."

"I am sure that many women would have loved you just because you are you," Weena pointed out.

David smiled.

"My family is somewhat like your brother, they are terribly impressed with people's titles and, if I had married someone without one, it would have been a *misalliance*. I am quite sure that my family would have done their best to oppose it."

He had said all this the other night when they were talking.

And it was this conversation that had decided her that she must tell him the truth.

If she married him on a lie, it would haunt her for the rest of her life.

Therefore after they had been to the ballet and held hands while the music seemed to envelop them as if it was a voice from Heaven, they had gone back to his house in Park Lane.

It was where everything was already arranged for the Reception after their wedding had been solemnised at St. George's Church in Hanover Square.

David took Weena into the study.

It was the only room that was not filled with the magnificent presents they were continually receiving.

"I must have one room," he had said, "which is free from white flowers and the scent of them where I can write a letter without knocking over a wedding present!"

"I must not keep you up late," David was saying as they entered the study. "You have a busy day tomorrow and I want you to look so beautiful on our wedding day that everyone there will think, as I do, that I am the luckiest man in the world."

"David, I have – something to – tell you," Weena began, stumbling over her words.

"What is it?" he asked.

"Something that – may prevent you from loving me and perhaps – from marrying me."

"What are you talking about?" David asked. "My darling Weena, what can have upset you? What has made you say that?"

"I know now," she said hesitatingly, "that – I just cannot marry – you telling a lie. Your sisters have told me how thrilled they are – that you are marrying someone they approve of."

She paused and took a deep breath before she went on,

"They were frightened – that you would be snapped up by a common woman who was only impressed by your title."

"They have no right to say such nonsense to you," David said. "What could be a lie when you tell me that you would love me whoever I was. It is what I was always seeking, but thought I would never find."

"I would love you as I love you now – if you were just plain David Hart," she told him. "But I have impressed your sisters and your other relations because they think – I am a Princess."

"Naturally they are impressed," he admitted, "but it does not affect us one way or another."

"Are you quite sure of that?" Weena asked.

"Of course I am. Why should you ask such a stupid question?"

Weena drew in her breath.

"Because," she said in a voice he could hardly hear, "I am not – a real Princess."

For a moment there was silence.

Then David asked,

"What do you mean?"

"Papa would never bother to follow up – the titles which were in his Family Tree," Weena said. "Mama was English and – as you know – came from a very respected English family. It never worried her that – although Papa was a big landowner and – had a magnificent collection of pictures and other treasures – he had never called himself a Prince and therefore neither Ivor nor I have a right to our – titles."

As she finished speaking, having stumbled over the words, she closed her eyes.

She felt that David might walk out of the room and that would be the last time she would ever see him.

Then to her immense surprise he laughed.

"So you hoodwinked all the snobs in Mayfair," he said, "including the Prince of Wales, who sent us a special wedding present today. My darling Weena, if you are not a Princess, you behave and look exactly like one."

He put his arms round her and turned her face up to his.

"I love you," he said. "I love you for telling me the truth. We must not let anyone know of it because of Ivor and his future father-in-law who is dancing up and down with unbounded joy as his daughter will be a celebrity in America."

"You are not angry – with me?" Weena whispered.

"I just love you and adore you even more than I did before," David replied. "To me you will always be not only a Princess but the Queen of my heart. I know we will be blissfully happy for the rest of our lives."

"How can you say such – wonderful things to me?" Weena asked and the tears were running down her cheeks.

David drew her closer to him and kissed away the tears.

Then he kissed her lips.

"I love you and I adore you," he said, "and I respect you for telling me the truth. It's a secret between the three of us and we will never talk about it again."

He paused for a moment before he added,

"The only thing I want you to realise is that I love you more every moment. When we are married, I know we will both live in a Heaven of our own where we will be ecstatically happy for the rest of our lives."

"My darling, darling David," Weena sighed, "you have rescued me by love no less than three times and now our love is more beautiful than a golden sunset and like the sunset it will last for ever."

Then he was kissing her, kissing her until she felt as though she was no longer herself but a part of him.

Nothing and no one could ever divide them.

*

They were married two days later at St. George's Church, Hanover Square.

151

After the Reception was over, they joined David's yacht which was waiting near the Houses of Parliament.

As it sailed majestically down the Thames and into the North Sea, Weena waited for her husband in the Master cabin which was filled with flowers.

Not only were they white but there were small pink roses and blue forget-me-nots.

The cabin was so beautiful that Weena felt as if she was living in a dream.

Later when David held her close in his arms, there was only the lap of the waves against the sides of the yacht.

She thought that she had somehow reached Heaven and the difficulties and troubles of the earth were no longer with them.

"I love you, I love you," she whispered to David.

"I will always adore and worship you, my beautiful wife," David murmured. "Now you are mine, completely mine and I will never lose you."

Then he was kissing her again.

As he made her his, he swept her up into the sky and she could hear the angels singing.

She felt that the love they shared was a part of God and came from God.

And it would be theirs for all Eternity.